2050

A WARNING

Richard Samulis

CROOK
BOOKS

Published by CROOK BOOKS

33/17 Eden Street, Adelaide, South Australia 5000

Copyright © Richard Samulis 2024

First Published 1st February 2024

Author: Samulis, Richard 1951-

Title: **2050 A WARNING**

This is a work of fiction, and any similarity to real people is entirely coincidental, with the exception of public figures and known organisations mentioned. Whilst mention is made of actual historical events, no aspersions are cast or intended in relation to any individuals for their part in those events. References to places and events are intended to reflect the author's opinions and impressions of real places.

A catalogue record for this work is available from the National Library of Australia

With heartfelt thanks to Dell for her enduring encouragement, to David Tregear for his valuable suggestions and typo corrections, Paul Coxon and Phil Page for their constructive reviews, and to Anne Tonkin for her many suggestions!

The views expressed in this book are solely those of the author.

"Do one thing every day that scares you."
— ELEANOR ROOSEVELT

"The big lesson in life, baby, is never be scared of anyone or anything."
— FRANK SINATRA

PROLOGUE

This book is a radical departure from my previous fictional stories of crime. I have become increasingly troubled by the path that Western culture has been following, so I'm going to tell you a different kind of story. You may consider it as a work of fiction, which after all, it is. But it is not only that. The events I am about to describe are intended as a basic warning of potential sequelae.

1

The summons shattered Adam's sense of serenity and order. As a news scriptwriter for the Buro, he was hard at work in conversation with his screen when a message overrode the display, flashing angrily in red. It said:

> *"ATTENDANCE REQUEST.*
> *WHERE? The Buro, 1 Victory Street.*
> *WHEN? Tomorrow. Wednesday 23RD February 2050 : 10 AM*
> *Please confirm acceptance."*

In all his twelve years with the Buro, this had never happened before. His stress level skyrocketed and his mouth parched. He knew he had no choice in the matter, so after clearing his throat he spoke: "Yes, I'll be there." The message disappeared, to be replaced briefly by an emerald-green *"Thank you. We look forward to seeing you,"* immediately followed by a fresh entry in his screen calendar.

Adam sat frozen, as all thoughts of the story he'd been working on evaporated. His imagination ran riot as he slowly and inexorably descended into a state of fear and dread. He forced himself to breathe deeply, and after a few minutes he managed to get a grip on his emotions. His rational mind overrode his feelings as he started to run various scenarios through his mind. *Is the Buro not satisfied with my output? Have I not been creative enough? Are my stories lacking in credibility? Have I inadvertently allowed feelings of negativity to seep through? But surely they would have said something in warning before now. But ... maybe it is good news! Maybe they plan to promote me. That is always possible.*

And then a terrifying thought crossed his mind. *Are they planning to replace me with an AI bot?*

His heart sank at the prospect, for he was not a brave man. Over the years, he'd tried not to think too much about that possibility, even though in the dark recesses of his mind, he knew it was inevitable. It was obvious that bots were taking over more and more of the functions previously handled by humans. They just got better and better at it. And whenever he found himself contemplating it, he'd always managed to shut it out of his mind because the ramifications were just too awful.

Adam, as a person who had access to the AI system and all of its genuine fact-checking, was in a highly privileged position and therefore high-status. He was trusted — up to a point — and there was rarely any time pressure on him to publish, because his news stories were generally fictitious and thus not particularly time-critical. And the Buro certainly

knew how to look after its own. They had been good
to him. Even after Adam's wife had died four years
previously they'd arranged his move to a somewhat
smaller apartment which was just as luxurious and
still quite large. In fact, in some ways he actually
preferred the new apartment, with its high ceilings
and its extensive use of pale marble, mahogany and
brass. It was very fitting as a 'gentleman's home,' as
he increasingly thought of himself. The Buro
arranged for a cleaner to come in once a week, on
Mondays as it happened, so it was no real bother for
him to keep the apartment clean and tidy.

He got up, fixed himself a scotch on the rocks and
then sat on his large soft leather sofa. But he couldn't
settle. He was afraid. He downed the rest of his
scotch, got up and fixed himself another and then sat
down again.

He was not especially prone to loneliness, which
was a lucky coincidence as he had no real friends, but
he could have used a friend right now. Someone to
tell him how silly he was being. No need to worry.
Things like that. His job was not conducive to
spending much time with people, and sometimes his
apartment started to feel a bit like a luxurious prison,
which is why he made a habit of going out for a coffee
or two each day. But there was no one with him now.
No one to stop him preparing for the worst.

It was four years ago that Evelyn died, and it seemed to Adam like yesterday. He'd never been able to reconcile things in his own mind. He had found her on the kitchen floor, laid out very neatly on her back with her centreline perfectly aligned with the kitchen work surfaces, as though by design. Her arms were folded over her belly and the only thing that betrayed the fact that she had been murdered was the knife handle protruding from her chest above her heart. There was surprisingly little blood. The Buro police had attended the scene and removed her body. There was never any funeral and no one ever told Adam what had happened to her. His sporadic attempts to gain information were fobbed off with various bland statements, along the lines of 'The Buro is still investigating.' Adam could not be sure that Evelyn's murder wasn't a warning to him, or that perhaps it was a raw demonstration of the power they had over him. But maybe, as another employee of the Buro, Evelyn had transgressed somehow. Adam had no idea what her job was, as she had never been willing to discuss it. Perhaps her job was to spy on him.

So Adam had responded by keeping his head down and not doing anything that might be considered controversial. Never one to confront a situation, he told himself that it was none of his business, a feat which required considerable emotional gymnastics. And when they moved him to his new apartment he soon started to think of himself as a successful and well-regarded bachelor. He tried very hard to not think about his Evie. After all, she was gone and he was not normally one to dwell on the past. But as you already know, he was not a particularly courageous man and it was never any use — images of his discovery of his poor dead Evie had a nasty habit of replaying themselves over and over again. His walls would always come crashing down around him. That night, he drank too much whisky.

―――――――――

Adam's dream encompassed the sound of his grandfather clock striking seven times in the distance, with a musical 'dong' sound. With each passing chime his mind tried to make sense of the sound. He imagined it as a car horn, and then a freight train until he awoke with a start and it all became clear.

He swung his feet around to sit on the edge of the bed, and rubbed his eyes. Something was wrong. And then a sense of dread returned as he realised that today was *the day*. It was not helped at all by a mild hangover, so he headed to the bathroom for a shave and a shower. He was startled when he accidentally caught sight of his haunted reflection staring right back at him. His blonde locks were sticking up all over the place, and the mirror exaggerated his freckles. He couldn't go to the Buro looking like that! A careful shave followed by a long, hot shower served to revive him, and as he towelled himself down afterwards he started to feel considerably better. His thoughts turned to the meeting, and he tried to discard all negative thoughts. He had to remain as upbeat as possible. Number one Victory Street was less than a kilometre away. He would need to allow, say twenty five minutes for the walk and he should plan to arrive ten minutes early. So he would need to leave at 9:25AM at the latest. It was in his nature to be organised and to plan ahead.

He opened his jocks drawer, selected a pair and donned them. Likewise some socks. He wasn't so used to wearing suits, but he did have three of them for such occasions. He selected a dark blue pinstripe and a white shirt. He buttoned up his loose-fitting shirt easily enough and inserted a pair of gold cufflinks, but when it came to his suit, it felt as though he'd put on a bit of weight since he'd last worn it. No matter, it still looked the part. He chose a golden yellow and navy-blue diagonally striped silk tie which he believed made him look like a true professional, and capped it off with a pair of expensive but plain shiny black-leather shoes. As he looked at the final effect in his full-length mirror, he suddenly felt overwhelmed at the prospect of the impending meeting. He felt like a fraud, out of his depth. Nausea came on, and he had to rush to the toilet to vomit. But nothing came up apart from clear fluid. Just a panic attack. It had been a while since he'd had one, but he knew full well what it was. After a few more deep breaths he felt more settled, so he headed for the kitchen to take on some ballast in the form of two fried eggs on toast.

2

9:25AM arrived. He took a deep breath and walked to his front door, which sensed his presence and glided open. He stepped out of his apartment into a clean, wide corridor and the door glided shut behind him. His apartment building was reserved for various high-status individuals, and the décor reflected that, with lavish use of marble and polished brass. He decided to take the stairs down. After all he was a fit-enough thirty-eight-year old, and his apartment was only three floors up. As he reached the ground level, a wheeled robot in the lobby was busying itself washing and blow-drying the marble floor, a small area at a time so as not to create any hazard for humans. The bot was showing its age somewhat, but the Buro had a strict replacement policy, and as long as it continued to do its job reliably, recycling could wait for another day.

A set of tall glass doors that led to the street slid open as Adam approached. He walked out of the building, hesitating for a moment at the top of the front steps to the building, just to soak up the atmosphere. No one paid him any heed, and why would they? He was just an ordinary-looking well-dressed guy, not too tall, not too short, quite slim, tousled blonde hair. There was nothing out of place about him, apart from his orange-framed spectacles, which he felt made him look interesting. He thought of them as his trademark and he was completely unaware of their vague incongruity against his necktie.

He jumped down the steps, three at a time and strolled up Victory Street towards the Buro's local offices. The street was very elegantly laid out, with wide granite pavements and a strip of cobblestones in the centre where driverless taxi modules slowly ferried people along. Four parallel rows of well-trimmed trees stretched off into the distance, and along the way were several coffee shops and pavement restaurants, interspersed with prestige accommodation blocks and the occasional office.

Adam arrived somewhat sooner than expected. It was now 9:45AM, so he just stood outside, looking at the imposing building with its massive columns and absurdly tall portico. It was certainly designed to impress and intimidate. It had pride of place as the first Victory Street address, sitting on the corner of a large public square called Triumph Plaza. Adam knew that the building was essentially a prefab, machined off-site in factories and then brought to site for assembly — which was largely done by robots. All very efficient. And despite it being a prefab, it certainly overachieved on its design objectives.

People were coming and going from the building intermittently, and almost all were wearing business suits. Mostly Buro staff, Adam assumed.

He waited outside until 9:53AM before nerves got the better of him. He decided to just get it over and done with, so he climbed the set of granite steps and walked into the open portico. There was a plinth opposite, with two stylish sculpted heads, one at each end and Adam immediately recognised it as an automated reception. As he approached the plinth, a voice said, "Welcome to the Buro, Mr Adam Brandon. Please proceed to Lift G." A heavy timber door to one side of the reception plinth slid open, and Adam walked through, to be confronted with a bank of perhaps twenty lifts, arranged into two corridors with lifts at either side. He followed the signs directing him towards Lift G, and as he approached, the doors swung open. He entered and the doors closed behind him. Suddenly he was overcome with fear again, so he breathed deeply and slowly. There was only a small delay before could sense that the lift was moving, very quietly, though he could not tell if it was going up or down. The lift soon became completely silent and after a short delay the doors slid open to reveal a fairly small dimly-lit room with no windows. The walls were mahogany panelled, but very austere with no ornamentation. Adam turned to look around, and saw that there was only the one lift door behind him. He just stood there, wondering what to do. Then after a moment, the timber panelling opposite the lift parted with a faint rumble to reveal a very large office beyond, which was completely symmetrical, and completely windowless. The whole office was also clad in mahogany but in contrast to the lift lobby employed elaborate architectural forms, one side being the mirror-image of the other. The floor was covered in a deep red, plain wool carpet.

Adam entered tentatively, feeling somewhat intimidated. A disembodied female voice said, "Welcome Mr Adam Brandon. Please take a seat in the leather chair." There was only one leather chair in the office, which was placed on the centreline with its back towards the main doors. It almost felt like a courtroom with the chair for the accused. Adam sat down. He looked up to take in the details and realised that there was a man seated four or five metres away, and at least two metres above him, in what could best be described as a kind of throne. He had not noticed him at all until that moment. The throne was protected by a massive timber bench between Adam and the man. At least he assumed it was a man. He was quite dimly-lit, and was wearing black robes and geometric head gear. His lower face was covered in a black cloth mask, similar to the ones used in the covid days, so it was really only his eyes that showed. Perhaps it was a bot, a possibility that served to disturb Adam even more. It spoke.

It said, "Welcome to the Buro, Mr Adam Brandon." Its voice was surprisingly high-pitched, which served to disorient Adam even more. It continued, "I trust your journey was not too arduous?"

Adam was not sure if the question was seriously intended, so he gave it the benefit of the doubt and replied, "No, it was an easy walk, thank you."

It then said, "I am gratified to hear it. The Buro's plan seems to be very effective, does it not?"

Adam guessed that it was meant as a statement rather than a question, so he acquiesced by replying, "Yes, sir. Indeed it does."

The man said, "You may call me Mr Curzon. Do you enjoy your work, Mr Brandon?"

"Thank you, yes Mr Curzon, very much."

"Which aspects in particular?

Adam had to stop and think for a moment. "I like the creative aspect. It allows me to support the vision that the Buro has for us all."

"And how would you describe that vision?"

"Peace and prosperity for all. Convenience, orderliness."

"I see. And do you have any views on how you would best manage society?"

Adam's alarm bells rang loud and clear. This was dangerous territory. "What do you mean, Mr Curzon?"

"I mean, do you have any views on how to best control society? Come on man, it's not a difficult question," he replied, somewhat testily.

"I don't know what you mean by that, sir. No one needs to be controlled. The Buro takes care of us all." As soon as the words left his mouth, he knew he'd misspoken. He had been too eager to please, in answering Mr Curzon with what he thought he wanted to hear. But it was part of his job description to assist the Buro in controlling people through the selective use of information and disinformation, and he realised he had to correct his error.

Mr Curzon replied with obvious impatience, "Oh, come now Mr Brandon! A man with your creative skills can do better than that! There are no wrong answers here."

A mounting fear and confusion took over and overwhelmed Adam. He knew he was in deep trouble, but could not bring himself to use the right words to rectify things. He could not think straight. It was like being in the middle of a terrible dream where he was struggling to run away, only to find that his legs would not respond. All remaining vestiges of bravery deserted him, and now his mind froze altogether, rendering him incapable of finding the words to break his silence. So he sat for some time, despairing, but in the back of his mind knowing that at some point it would all be over. He continued to sit, mind frozen. Maybe for only a few seconds, but more likely for a minute or two.

And then Mr Curzon broke the stillness with, "Very well, you may go now." The shock of hearing Mr Curzon's voice again woke Adam out of his reverie.

"Excuse me?"

"The meeting is over. Thank you for attending."

Adam froze with fear again. It was impossible to read Mr Curzon's face. And it was difficult to even see where Mr Curzon was looking. He seemed to be reading something, perhaps in readiness for the next meeting. There was only one way for this nightmare to end, and that was to walk out. So Adam forced himself to get up and bow slightly, before turning and walking back from whence he'd come. His mind was screaming for a reset. Another chance. A rewind. But the mahogany doors slid shut behind him and the lift opened its doors. He stepped in, and after a few moments he was deposited back on the ground floor. He stepped out and made for the heavy timber door he'd used when he first arrived. As he approached, it opened silently, and he stepped out to the portico. No one bid him farewell, or thanked him for coming. It was as though he'd ceased to matter.

3

He knew that he had just been assessed — and found wanting. He knew himself well enough to know that the last thing he needed now was to be left alone with his own thoughts. He needed people around him. Anything to give him a sense of normality, to forget the horror show he'd just witnessed himself orchestrating. He needed a coffee at his usual spot close to his apartment on Victory Street, to calm himself with its familiarity. It was mainly a pavement café with a very small interior but it had plenty of outside seating under a canopy of grapevines. For rainy days, they had a clever arrangement of cascading glass panels which kept it all nice and dry below. As he arrived at the café, quite unusually there were almost no seats free. He cast his eyes around and spotted a two-seat table at the far end, so he hurried towards it to claim it. He sat, feeling pleased that he'd managed it, as there were others milling around looking for a suitable table.

In the centre of each table was an embedded touch screen, and as the table recognised Adam, he was just asked to confirm his 'usual', which he did. The coffee would then be made by a human barista, delivered by robot and payment taken from his personal account without any further demands being made on him. All very convenient. The owner, a woman named Wilhelmina Block kept an eye on things and mingled occasionally, whenever the fancy took her. One could easily spot her with her startling head of bushy white hair and her rotund figure. She was far too young to have earned her shock of white hair, but she didn't bother dyeing it, perhaps because it contrasted so becomingly with her olive skin. She had been a benign presence at the café ever since anyone could remember. Rumour had it that it was the shock of her husband and child being killed in an accident that turned her hair white overnight. Adam had no idea if the rumours were true or not, as he'd never taken the trouble to look them up, but in any case, he'd only been coming to her café for a few years and it did not matter to him either way.

His coffee soon arrived, brought to him by a humanoid robot with legs. The older generation of wheeled bots were always a problem, as every ripple in the pavement tended to result in spilt coffee. This new breed solved that problem perfectly with their uncanny ability to avoid so much as a ripple on the surface of the coffee.

Adam took his first sip with pleasure and gratitude, and then placed the cup back on the saucer. The ritual of it all soothed and calmed him. He allowed his world to open up and he became aware of a woman standing near his table. He looked up at her and saw that she was peering around for a free table. On the spur of the moment he invited her to join him. That was quite out of character for Adam — far too personal an act — but when he later replayed the events in his mind, he realised that it was simply because he needed people around him. For comfort. A distraction from his woes. To help take his mind off them.

At first, she seemed a little hesitant, and asked, "Are you sure you don't mind?" to buy herself some time to size Adam up. She decided he looked normal enough, handsome even despite his orange glasses, so she beamed at him as she said, "Thank you. That's very kind of you. I've never known this place to be so busy, have you?" As she sat down Adam didn't want to make her feel in any way obligated, so he said simply, "No, it's very unusual, isn't it?" and said no more.

While she selected her coffee from the touch screen, he made his own quick assessment. She was probably a few years older than him, also wearing an expensive business suit. Her hair was very dark and her skin was creamy. Overall, a face that would grow on you.

She looked up and said, "By the way, my name is Penny."

"Adam," he replied with a smile.

"What do you do?" she asked. There was little point in lying about it, so he replied, "I'm a news scriptwriter." That seemed to surprise Penny. Her eyes widened, then immediately narrowed. "For the Buro?" she asked warily.

"Yes, that's right," replied Adam, matter-of-factly.

"Oh, I see," she said, and an awkward silence descended. That was often the reaction he got when people found out his occupation and he realised it was up to him to make her feel at ease, so after a moment he asked her what she did. She explained that she was a theoretical mathematician, working on human-machine interfacing. In other words, AI robots! That revelation stopped Adam in his tracks somewhat. The best response he could come up with was, "Wow. I never would have guessed. It sounds very technical, is it?" He was careful enough not to betray his feelings about bots.

"Yeah, you could say that. Most of what I do is developing AI algorithms to try to encourage bots to think for themselves. The holy grail is achieving self-awareness. But it's a bit like chasing after something that always seems to be five years away!" She paused, expecting some sort of comment from Adam, but none was forthcoming, so she changed topic. "But your work sounds interesting too. How did you get involved?"

Just then, Penny's coffee arrived, and Adam used the distraction to get his thoughts together. He wasn't sure what to think of Penny's revelation. She was involved in making bots creepier and creepier. He stared slightly open-mouthed for a moment until he realised she was waiting for his response, so he brought himself back to earth and replied, "Oh, nothing I do is as impressive as your work. After I completed my psychology degree, I started applying for jobs and I fully expected to finish up in clinical practice. That was what I was interested in. I was particularly fascinated by how easily people can be manipulated by fear. You know, fear as a tool."

Penny stiffened with those words, but Adam failed to notice as he was not watching her face right then. He was distracted by his own thoughts. But then he returned his gaze to her eyes and continued, "There weren't so many jobs about then. Anyway, after a couple of years of living on a Universal Basic Income, I was approached by the Buro and offered a job as a trainee news scriptwriter. Trainee News Screenwriters, we called them back then." There was something about Penny that encouraged him to say more than he really wanted. He found himself adding, "I suppose it's now become a real art form." He hesitated, to check himself from saying too much. Penny was watching him like a hawk, preparing to ask a question that needed to be asked.

"And does your art form include the use of fear?"

Adam immediately realised he'd said too much already. Penny's question was too close to the bone for comfort, and Adam cursed himself for being too open to Penny's charms. He tried to put his guard up again, but was suddenly overwhelmed with flashes of his disastrous meeting with Mr Curzon. His thoughts became a jumbled mess. He just wanted to cry. He took a deep breath or two to calm himself, to regain his composure. He felt rotten and distraught as he blurted out, "I'm sorry to say ... I think I'll soon be for the high jump because of your work. It can't be long now before bots take over." At that, Penny's face showed a touch of distress, so he added, "I'm sorry, don't worry, I'm not critical of your work. I know that we can't stop progress."

He had ducked Penny's question and she knew it. But she also saw a tortured, conflicted soul before her. She felt a bit sorry for him on the one hand, but knew that he had all but confirmed that he did indeed use fear as a weapon, and that disgusted her.

Adam took a few more deep breaths, and as he calmed himself he added, as cheerily as he could muster, "Oh look, I'm just being a bit paranoid. Tell me more about bots. There seem to be more of them on the streets with each new day that goes by. I'm actually very interested. Please!"

Penny raised her eyebrows. She no longer approved of or trusted Adam, but she kept up polite appearances as she replied, "Oh really, that isn't my area of expertise. I just work on the interfaces, and I have nothing to do with deploying any bots. That's more to do with the strategy people at the Buro. But yes, you're right. There does seem to be more of them about. And I'm sorry if it offends you, but I'm actually very proud to be part of it, because with every new generation they just become so much better. Look at how far we've come in the last twenty or thirty years. They've moved from being pretty crude, very obviously mechanical devices, to the latest models being almost indistinguishable from humans, if you ignore the aesthetics. There are not many jobs these days that they're not capable of, so that frees people up from all sorts of drudgery. It allows them to fulfil their potential. Maybe that's the way to look at it in your position."

Adam could have said all sorts of things in response to that, few of them complimentary, so he refrained from saying anything at all. He adopted what he thought was a benign smile, though she read it as a grimace. He knew from his own work how difficult it could be to get people to think for themselves, or show any signs of being able to adapt. In fact most people didn't seem to want to put any intellectual effort in at all. It was easier just to have faith in the Buro. They would look after your best interests! Wouldn't they?

Penny, now quite uncomfortable, suddenly glanced at her watch, and said, "Oh hell! I've got to go! Very nice talking to you Adam, but I must make tracks. Maybe see you around!" And then she was gone. Adam hoped he hadn't offended her and driven her off — but he knew he had.

4

A few days came and went without any contact from the Buro. There was no follow-up from the meeting. Nothing at all. Adam knew he was always prone to think the worst, so he cast it out of his mind as best he could, and just got on with his job. He was working on several news stories at the same time, and as he got a bit stuck with the creative aspects of one story, he'd work on another and then pick up the original story later. He found it stretched him well enough. But in the days following that awful meeting, he began suffering from feelings of pointlessness, as though he were missing a sense of purpose. And although he tried to cast aside all memories of the meeting, there was no one to offer any comfort, and those memories kept returning to overwhelm him as he struggled to get his emotions back on an even keel.

It was no use. He gave up on his attempts to write, got up from his chair and went into his sitting room for a change of scenery. He decided he deserved a nice cold beer in order to comfort himself, so he opened the bar fridge door, took out a bottle and a chilled glass and poured one into the other. After all, everyone needs comforting from time to time. He sat down on his beautiful oversized Chinese brocade sofa to relax and soon found himself reflecting on his life. He'd seen such massive changes, but his life was missing something. And it wasn't only his Evie. There were painful periods when he still missed her like crazy, and he struggled to put those awful images of her murder out of his mind, but it wasn't just that. Since that meeting, he began to feel as though his life had been a total fraud. It all seemed so pointless. Being the cerebral man that he was, he drifted into reflecting on his past in an attempt to resolve his tortured feelings — though maybe he was also being a tad self-indulgent.

He was an eight-year-old schoolboy at the time that the covid pandemic hit, and he only had sketchy memories of anything before that. He remembered having to stay at home for his schooling and not being allowed to go outside. And having to mask up in public, which disturbed him a lot. He felt trapped and surrounded by expressionless aliens. His parents did everything to look after him, but it seemed to go on forever. He learnt to be very wary of the power that others had over him. The authorities seemed to be able to do whatever they wanted, and there was no choice but to comply. And then, suddenly the pandemic was all over bar the shouting.

The next strong memory was when he was fourteen, when the Big Black wreaked havoc. There were major electricity shortfalls, which led to electrical power rationing and major blackouts, sometimes at random and sometimes according to a published schedule. That led to a major recession (some called it a depression) a year or so later and it was a very black time in all senses, until it petered out when he was eighteen. Now that he was a privileged Buro employee with full access to the AI system and its fact-checking, he'd been able to go back and research what had actually happened. He found that before the Big Black, there was a generally accepted view that the earth was slowly warming, and it was all because of increasing atmospheric carbon dioxide. There were two things that changed that view. Politics and Science.

As the wilder predictions on the climate were simply not coming to pass, vested interests like the IPCC attempted to ramp up the fear factor by increasingly absurd predictions. But as the rhetoric became more and more extreme in an attempt to instil fear into the populace, it inevitably dawned on people that reality was not matching the fear-mongering. Cynicism was taking root with ordinary people. And among scientists, there was a creeping realisation that their projections and predictions were not coming to fruition — they were confusingly wide of the mark. Of course, that was not enough to give any pause to the absolute certainty of the political classes. After all, very many people now depended financially on keeping the official narrative going, so it had to be protected by fair means or foul. Businesses were being coerced into making supportive statements on pain of losing their green credentials. ESG took root, forcing companies to do business solely with others who had similarly signed up to the new regime. There were rumours that Governments were employing arsonists to set fires which fed into the catastrophic climate change narrative. Universities became utterly corrupted as the younger, indoctrinated generation took over the reins and closed their minds to any views other than the 'received wisdom.' And then credentialed 'experts' came to the fore, paid to support whatever agenda the powerful decided was in their own best interests.

It was all too much. An over-reach. Gradually at first, the narrative started to fall apart. One by one the braver members of the scientific community could no longer live with the bullying and scientific dishonesty. They overcame their fear of losing funding and wrote articles explaining that increasing carbon dioxide levels were nothing to be feared, that current levels were at historic lows, and that a dose of warming would be quite beneficial in any event. The first of them did indeed lose their funding and were treated as pariahs. But the truth, inconvenient as it was, gained a hold. After all, what is science without truth? Soon, one rebel gave courage to another, and it built slowly to become an avalanche of support. They began to publish their calculations showing that a logarithmic effect meant there would only be minimal further warming and that the increasing level of carbon dioxide was actually encouraging plant growth and increasing crop yields. The earth was greening. All this coincided with a run of exceptionally cool summers and it turned out that the earth had tipped into a long-term cooling phase. So the narrative was being undermined pretty rapidly.

But that was still not enough. Science became increasingly disconnected from politics and vested interests. For a long time after scientists had started to raise their concerns, western governments were still legislating to ban the use of fossil fuels in a push towards 'Net Zero' with the intention of making the use of 'renewable' energy sources the only economically viable option: all to protect their investments. At the same time, they were busy legislating for EV's — electric vehicles — which increased the demand for electricity even more. There was a looming electricity shortfall, and the signs were there for all to see. But governments turned a blind eye — some of the more honourable individuals out of ignorance — but they continued to use fear as a weapon, and were cashing in on the bonanza.

At the same time, there was a dawning understanding amongst the more enlightened politicians and amongst the business community that there were simply not enough metal and mineral resources to supply the projected demand. So the question of recycling reared its ugly head, but soon went straight into the 'too hard' basket.

And then the Big Black changed everything.

Western governments, having driven fossil fuel power generation largely out of existence, at first tried to pretend that there was no issue with electricity supply. But reality intervened and, slowly to begin with, the blackouts became more frequent and less predictable. Within months it became impossible to gloss over the blackouts, especially when businesses were badly affected. So people started taking to the streets in protest, and their numbers increased rapidly. Some governments tried to marginalise the protesters by planting 'extremist' groups among them, whose job it was to be violent and thus sully the reputation of the protesters *pour décourager les autres*. That only worked for a while until people worked out what was going on, and by then it was too late to stop the Big Black getting worse and worse. Governments everywhere were under attack and were themselves frightened. There was a big push towards nuclear power as the only truly Net-Zero-friendly power source, but the construction lead times were so long that they could offer no short term relief. People *en masse* stopped paying their exorbitant electricity bills, food chains were interrupted because of the power shortages for transport, and communities everywhere were days away from chaos.

So in a radical act of self-preservation, everything went into reverse quite suddenly. Politicians ditched their 'firm positions', and instead there was a mad flurry to do whatever it took, including re-instigating the use of fossil fuels. They suddenly found the courage to ignore any concern for 'political correctness.' After all it was their heads on the block. The first back on line was gas, but the closing of coal mines was also reversed, and efforts to bring nuclear plants back online continued apace as new ones were being built.

It was still not enough. A societal collapse was underway. Increasingly drastic control measures were needed. It was the USA that set the precedent in declaring martial law, but others quickly followed. *Les autres* were *encouragés*. Safety in numbers.

China prevaricated and then decided to take advantage of the weakness of the West to invade Taiwan. The leadership calculated that with the west so embroiled in their own problems, Taiwan would fall in a matter of days, and so end 'the hundred years of humiliation.' Things didn't work out that way. The USA had supplied most of the weaponry in the Hamas invasion of Israel a couple of years previously, and its stocks were rapidly replaced with up to date weaponry. The Chinese were not so lucky, and all of the weaknesses inherent in the Chinese military command soon led to all sorts of disarray. History shows that the Western nations, though initially slow to react, were able to muster overwhelming, battle-hardened forces against China, which quickly crumbled. Experience made the difference. Russia made noises about joining the war, but they were dealing with the aftermath of the bloody war with Ukraine and so were no practical help to any side. And by the time they were ready (assuming they ever intended to join), it was all over. In the terms of surrender, China had been forced to accept a demilitarised zone extending for five hundred kilometres from Taiwan. It was a sorry tale of thwarted ambition.

Even before that war was over, the ineffectualness of the weaker governments was laid bare for all to see. And people knew they had been misled and lied to. There was a complete breakdown in trust for institutions. National governments seemed incapable of addressing anyone's needs, and so started to form local alliances. But they then fell under the spheres of influence of the largest among them including China, until there were only two left standing: 'the reds' and 'the alliance'. The reds formed their own defence and trading blocks to the exclusion of all others, partly because they now had no choice but to rule with an iron fist, and partly to hide the reality of life in those states. It was Cold War 2.0.

Gradually, the Big Black ended as more energy sources came online. But now, no one in government wished to go back to the old ways, even when they could have. They were far too drunk on the power and the excitement of it all. Of course, nobody asked the people what they wanted, because the answer was quite obvious. Although it has to be said, a growing number of the less able were pretty comfortable with the idea of the government running their lives and being the provider. That principal had been clearly established in the covid era, and the authorities had learnt that lesson well. It made the insecure feel secure. They had their 'Daddy' to look after them. So before long martial law was the norm, with all of the means of control implied by that and very few in government wanted to change anything. But it was never going to be sustainable or acceptable to keep on calling it 'martial law.' Some change had to be made. So treaties were signed, formalising the current arrangements though with a different name. Some of these treaties could be seen almost as a re-colonisation of much of the third world. A council of nations was formed, which formalised the new treaties with other supra-national bodies like the WHO and the UN, and it continued to incrementally assume more powers. Worst of all, it seemed that no one noticed or cared, because in all of this, the voice of the common man no longer mattered. Free speech was just a distant memory. Of course, everybody realised that the West was actually run by the USA, for the benefit of the USA, but the rules of the game were that as long as you pretended everything was just dandy, you would be looked after and all your needs taken care of, which on the face of it was an attractive enough bargain.

No one could quite agree on a name for the council of nations, and for some reason it became known unofficially as 'the bureau,' often misspelled as 'The Buro,' with the intention of giving it its permanent name at a later date when all could agree. But that day never arrived, so 'The Buro' stuck and the name became synonymous with 'the alliance'. And Adam tried to shut from his mind the fact that the Buro took advantage of every major event to increasingly restrict freedoms. To impose greater control.

The opposing 'reds' (who had implemented almost identical policies) were simply referred to as the Red Block, and demonised accordingly. Fear about the Red Block was sown deliberately, which was not such a difficult task after China's unsuccessful invasion of Taiwan. Constant news stories about the evil Red Block were created and published. After all, there is nothing as effective as having a common enemy to unite people. The irony of the situation was not lost on Adam, though he would never admit it openly. After all, he was now a primary contributor to it, and as his eyes slowly opened to it all, he understood full well that he was now part of the system. He had no choice but to go along with it — always assuming that he continued to be given that choice.

There were a few stray countries that remained independent — but only because no one cared much about them — and it was easy enough to restrict travel to those countries.

Once the Big Black petered out, power generation had reverted to mainly fossil fuels, although construction of new nuclear plants continued apace.

But there was a proliferation of solar panels covering vast swaths of land, and as they ceased to function they were not being replaced. That left a major clean-up of the defunct panels required. But it was not economic to do so, because it was very difficult and expensive to recycle them. So the countryside in those areas remained derelict-looking, but there was nothing stopping you from pretending to yourself that the fields were full of exotic silver-grey and black crops.

Windmills were a different issue. They had been installed pretty much anywhere deemed windy enough, but their lifespan was very poor. As they were taken offline, some enterprising companies disassembled them for salvage of their large quantities of copper. Most of the columns were made of steel, which was easily recycled. But some were made of concrete, which wasn't. So that left the fibreglass turbine blades, concrete columns and footings as waste, and they littered the landscape like broken, giant tin soldiers. But over time, people did get used to the mess or at least did not complain about it. And in any event most people were completely unaware of them, as a long time had gone by since they were free to travel to local beauty spots. There were no longer any private cars allowed. It was much easier to control people's movements that way. The Buro maintained the road network for its own use, so there were never any traffic jams and thus speed limits could be removed as per the 'autobahn' model.

Normal citizens had to either walk, or take a Personal Driverless Transport Module (officially known as PDTM's, but that was too much of a mouthful, so everyone just called them taxibots, or more commonly, just plain taxis.) They were paid for by distance travelled. Within the cities it was never a problem as no permissions were required, but for longer distance trips a spoken application was required before travel, and one needed a good reason to gain approval.

Adam took another swig of his beer, and got up to get another. Reminiscing and researching was hard work — it took its toll on the emotions! Things swirled in Adam's mind and despite his having already lived through such radical changes, a strong sense of foreboding permeated his soul — and it was not just his worries with the Buro. It was those damned bots. The newest ones were just plain creepy with their AI abilities. You could never be sure what they were thinking, nor whom they were watching. More than once Adam had caught the eye of a bot which immediately looked away, pretending not to be spying on him. Adam realised that they were a lot smarter than they pretended. And how could they be trusted? Nobody had any idea of whether they had any moral compass at all, but in the absence of evidence, it was a fair bet that they did not. They were dangerous, and no one seemed to notice that they were taking over, one step at a time. He had a palpable sense that the worst was yet to come. The time for the robots was surely approaching and no one was prepared.

5

The days added up, and soon a week had passed by with no contact from the Buro. Adam was starting to dismiss any thoughts about Mr Curzon from his mind. Everything was as normal, his work was going well and all seemed right in the world, and even his worries about bots faded from his consciousness. And it looked to be a beautiful sunny day outside, so he decided to go for a morning coffee. He paused at the top of the steps to his apartment building, as he often did, just to feel the day. It was perfectly sunny, not too warm and not too cold. His spirits lifted. Life was definitely worth living!

He walked over to the café, found a table easily enough and sat down. But the embedded touch screen showed nothing. Thinking it must have been faulty, he moved tables. Same thing. The table refused to recognise him. This made no sense at all. Adam had been cranially chipped during his final year at university as an early adopter, and had never had a problem with it since. It was a couple of years after that when it was made compulsory for all. So from then on at birth, one's digital identity was embedded and fixed for life, and all children and adults were required to be chipped, for everyone's convenience. After all, there were such huge benefits to be had. Everyone could easily be identified, so the crime figures plummeted. Taxation could be automatically deducted from one's account, so there was no longer a need for paperwork. Banking became so simple. Everything was controlled by the Buro, so anyone contemplating antisocial behaviour could simply be prevented from doing so by selectively blocking access to their funds or to their use of taxis. It was for everyone's benefit. Payment of Universal Basic Income entitlements became seamless. Healthcare records on individuals were instantly available, so the best possible health care was always given.

So you can imagine how distressing it was for Adam to lose his system recognition. He had never heard of such a 'failure to recognise' before now, and he simply did not know what to do. He looked around helplessly. Maybe he could talk to Wilhelmina Block, but thought better of it. He didn't want to embarrass her, and this was not something she could help with. He could either try to do something about it, or walk away and pretend this never happened.

He chose the latter. Less fuss that way. No need to draw attention to it. No need to make an issue of it. So he got up again and picked his way through the tables, and suddenly, there was Penny, sat looking at him open-mouthed. He wasn't sure if she had been trying not to notice him, but there was no avoiding it now, for either of them.

She smiled and said politely, "How nice to see you again, Adam. I haven't seen you around for a few days. Have you been busy?" Adam mumbled, "Yes, I have been a bit. Look I'm sorry. I'd join you, but it seems I'm suffering from a chip failure." Penny looked puzzled for a moment. She said, "I've never heard of that before. Do you mean you can't access your funds?" Adam nodded. Her human concern took over, and she added, "Oh, no need to worry. I'll buy your coffee. What would you like?"

He told her as he sat down. He was feeling very disoriented, but Penny seemed unfazed. He was not up to his usual standards of conversation (not that that's saying much), as he became preoccupied with his chip failure. His fear rose as he started to understand the implications. He became quite agitated at the thought that he may be locked out of his apartment. And if it weren't a chip failure, then that would just be the start of his worries. It would mean that he had transgressed somehow, and he knew in his bones that it would be because of his awful interview with Mr Curzon. There was nothing else.

So as soon as he was decently able, he thanked her for his coffee and made his way back home with bated breath. He ran up his apartment block steps two at a time. The front doors slid open on his approach. He felt the ecstasy of overwhelming relief. The next test was the lifts. No problem there either. And finally, as he approached his apartment door, it slid open in welcome.

He'd had a real fright. He went into his office and sprawled on his leather sofa, before deciding he needed a scotch on the rocks. So he got up and fixed himself one and flopped on his sofa again. He got to thinking. He needed to know what had failed. What had caused the table to ignore him. He asked his screen if there was a problem with any of his bank accounts, and it replied, "No." He thought for a moment, and then asked if there had been a problem with his chip, to which the screen replied, "No." So he thought about it for a while longer, and decided it must be to do with how you frame the question. So he asked if there had been any problems with anything to do with his identity. Same answer. "No."

The screen was lying to him, and he didn't know why. A shiver of fear went down his spine.

6

It was a loud knocking sound. At first, Penny did not register what was causing it, because it had been a few years since anyone had knocked on her front door. Then she realised what it was. Fear and worry, those two old bedfellows, came to the fore. She looked at her screen, and could see two men, one pretty big and one fairly slight, lined up in front of her door. As she was not expecting them or anyone else, she decided to enable a glass screen, which immediately descended outside her front door as a safety measure. She approached the door, which dutifully slid open leaving her separated from her two visitors only by the glass. The slight man spoke. He said, "Penny Jakes?" and continued as she nodded, "We are from the Citizen Protection Buro. May we come in please? We would like to clarify a few things." Penny held up her screen to them each in turn, and it verified them as Glenn Graham and Karl Petersen, both Buro Citizen Protection employees. So she allowed the glass screen to rise up, and the men entered her apartment one after the other and she ushered them to the room that doubled up both as a working space and a sitting room. Both men were somewhere around forty years old, clean shaven and wearing dark grey suits, white shirts and a slender black tie. The only point of differentiation was that Karl Peterson was larger and more thickset.

Hers was a small apartment, though it was in a prestigious area, two streets back from Victory Street. As a technical worker she was not deemed to be high risk, as almost all of her peers were happy to concentrate on their work and were never exposed to political matters. Sometimes it was necessary to remind them of the facts of life, but such occurrences were rare. Penny offered her guests a seat on a small two seat sofa which was the only one she had, and for herself she pulled up her office-style chair. "Now, how can I help you?"

The slender man, Glenn Graham spoke. "We understand that you met with a fellow by the name of Adam Brandon yesterday morning, and you bought him a coffee. This was the second time in a week that you had a coffee with him, although you each paid for your own the first time. But you did share the same table on both occasions. Would you be so kind as to explain in your own words, why you shared a table and why you bought him a coffee. Thank you."

Penny was horrified, though she maintained enough self-control that perhaps these Buro men did not guess what she was going through. She was utterly disoriented, as this was the first time that she had been confronted with the level of detail of her personal life that the Buro was prepared to examine.

But she explained as best she could, that a week ago, the café was unusually busy, so Adam had made an offer that she share his table. And that she had returned the favour the previous day when he seemed to be suffering from a chip failure of some sort. She was just trying to help him out, and it seemed to be of no importance at the time. There was no more to it than that!

The two men exchanged glances and continued to sit in silence for a while, which Penny found very disconcerting. Then Glenn Graham said, stone-faced, "OK, well thank you for your time, madam. We'll leave you to it," and got up. Karl Petersen had not said a word the whole time and remained silent as both men found their own way out. He didn't even thank her for her time. As they left, Penny was feeling quite distressed, and she resolved to avoid Adam like the plague if he showed up again. It would be best to avoid any trouble with the Buro.

7

In the early hours of the following morning Adam was having real trouble getting back to sleep. His world was falling apart before his very eyes. Figuratively speaking. *'What do they say? Take away a man's pillars of support, and his world is but moments away from collapse. Something like that, anyway'.* He glanced at his watch. 3:34AM. Suddenly a light went on. It was in the entry foyer which led to his bedroom. *'That's the first time that's happened. It must be a fault.'* He got up, pulled on a bath robe and went to investigate. He found two men were standing in the foyer. Adam was taken aback — shocked and shaken at the sight of them. He blurted out, "Can I help you gentlemen?"

Adam had never set eyes on the pair before but it was Glenn Graham and Karl Petersen. Glenn said mildly, "We're sorry for the intrusion, sir, but you need to accompany us right now."

Adam was frightened by now. "What do you mean? Who on earth are you? Why should I go with you?" Adam asked.

"No need to make a fuss sir, we're from the Buro," said Glenn, softly and persuasively, as he'd been trained to do. "It's just a routine enquiry. It will go much easier for you if you don't make a fuss."

Adam said, "Let me quickly get dressed," but Glenn replied gently, "No sir, there isn't the time."

Of course these were textbook tactics by the Buro, to make sure that Adam felt as vulnerable and disoriented as possible, to soften him up for what was to come. Adam knew that, and his sense of dread went sky-high. He was escorted out of his apartment barefoot, into the lift, across the foyer and down the front steps to an awaiting taxibot. The streets were dark and deserted, and it was quite cold. The two men placed Adam in the centre seat and sat either side of him. Adam remained silent; too afraid to ask why he had been arrested for fear of it being something serious. The taxi set off silently and made the short journey to Number 1 Victory Street. Rather than arriving at the front entrance, the taxi turned down the adjacent street to access the rear of the building, and then drove into the building down a ramp. It parked next to a set of lifts, and all three men got out and walked straight into a waiting lift, which closed its doors after them and started moving. As before, Adam could not tell if it was going up or down, but soon the doors opened again to reveal a poorly-lit painted concrete corridor. The floors were black, the walls an indeterminate green-blue, and the ceilings grey. Adam was sure they were several floors below ground and so he felt somewhat entombed. Glenn said softly, "To your left, please," so Adam sheepishly went to the left, down the two metre wide corridor, passing several doors along the way. Glenn was leading the trio by now, and stopped in front of another door, which seemed to be the same as any other door. It obligingly opened, revealing a concrete room of perhaps five metres square, with no defining features apart from a table and two chairs. Adam felt some relief that at least there wasn't any torture equipment in the room. Glenn offered Adam a chair, and so he sat. He felt at an acute disadvantage, as he was barefoot and completely naked under his bathrobe. At least he wasn't cold yet, but he knew that if he were to be here for any length of time, the bare concrete would soon chill his feet. Karl stood near the door and after a moment Glenn Graham sat on the other chair. He still did not make any introduction to either himself or Karl, and Adam was too frightened to ask. Glenn asked pleasantly, "Do you know why you are here, Mr Brandon?"

"No, I don't."

"Why do you think you are here?"

"I don't have the slightest idea."

"None at all? Surely now, Mr Brandon."

"Oh, well is it something to do with my interview at the Buro last week?"

"Oh, so you think it is? How do you think it went?"

"I don't know."

Glenn chuckled. "Come now. Do you think it went perfectly?"

"I suppose not."

"What would you have said differently, given the chance?"

Adam sat stonily. Glenn smiled encouragingly and spread his hands as if to say, "Well?"

A thought occurred to Adam. He felt he'd blown it when he said that no one needs to be controlled, and that the Buro would take care of everyone. *What if the Buro is giving me a chance to revise the answers I gave to Mr Curzon? Maybe they do value my output!* So he said in reply, "I was probably a bit glib in my original answer. As I recall, I was asked about the best ways to control people. There are actually a lot of ways that can be used to control people."

"Such as?"

"Well, by restricting the publication of certain information for example."

"Give me an example."

"Oh. I don't know. Anything that reflects poorly on the Buro."

The next thing that happened shocked Adam to his core. The previously mild-mannered Glenn Graham paused for a moment, and then screamed, absolutely screamed at full volume, "*For fuck's sake man, don't tell me what you think I want to hear. Tell me the truth!*" He let a few seconds pass before adding in a soft voice, "Just don't bullshit me, and we'll get along fine."

Adam had never felt so vulnerable and uncertain in his life. His feet were cold and he was humiliated. He just wanted it all to be over, so he resolved to just do whatever was asked. He said, "I'm sorry. Please ask me again and I'll try to answer properly."

Glenn fixed his eyes on him and said quietly, "OK, that's better. Let's discuss how you would go about controlling people, shall we?" He looked down, perhaps to collect his thoughts. "Let's talk about truth."

"Yes, well, there are as many varieties of truth as people on the planet. I see my rôle as steering people towards the desired opinions."

"You mean through the use of disinformation?"

"Yes, well. You could say that, I suppose. He who controls the narrative controls the people I guess. As I'm sure you're aware, there are several ways of influencing opinion. One way is to spin the truth to give a misleading impression. Another is to fabricate stories to confuse things, or to silence opponents for example. If a problematic story is already out there, then I try to sow doubt on the facts and at the same time, I mix it up with a few fabrications — enough so that people can't see through to the real story."

Adam paused. His words were causing him some disquiet, as though he were pretending to be something he was not. It was not sitting well with him. He looked to Glenn for affirmation, but Glenn gave no indication as to whether he was happy with this newfound truthfulness or not. So Adam continued, though his heart was not in it at all.

"Whenever I'm trying to silence an opponent, I try to stick to the truth as far as possible. That means researching anything and everything to do with that opponent and everyone around him or her, while looking out for things that can be twisted and used against them." A deep sadness descended on Adam as he added, "Some people are quite naïve and leave themselves very open to all sorts of accusations, and I try to take advantage of that. Most people just want to feel safe and secure, and it's easy enough to play on that by making the world seem a much more dangerous place than it actually is. So it's always best to create stories that give the impression of great danger out there. And one of the best ways is to know your audience, and make up several different stories that take opposite positions, to polarise them or confuse them. That divides people up very effectively, and makes them frightened of anyone not from their 'tribe', so if you then offer the safety umbrella of the Buro, they're predictably grateful."

Adam was having trouble reading Glenn's face, which was making him feel very uncomfortable. He could not tell how well his little speech was going down and needed some encouragement to keep going. As if reading his mind, Glenn said, "Please continue."

So Adam continued. "As you'll know, the best thing to unite people is having a common enemy. So in a way, my job is to make sure people always have a readily identifiable enemy." Adam paused to reflect, and then added, "You might not be aware that a few years back the Buro's planning department highlighted an impending food shortage which would have caused a whole heap of issues with social unrest. The ramifications would have been terrible. So the Buro decided that the only way to circumvent the shortage was to produce artificial food in factories. People got wind of the plans and were not at all happy about it, so we instigated a propaganda campaign to convince people that so-called 'natural' food was dangerous because it was riddled with bacteria and viruses and microbes and other nasties. We called factory food 'green food' and gradually people started seeing natural food as the enemy. That solved the problem and green food is used to this very day! I was very proud of my part in driving that campaign, because it was so effective."

Adam looked to Glenn for some form of approval, but none was forthcoming. Glenn's face betrayed nothing. Perhaps he didn't care, and was just doing his job. Adam glanced at Karl, who was giving a very good impression of being asleep on his feet, or perhaps he was just bored. Adam realised that he would have been exposed to a lot worse. This was probably child's play to the big man. Glenn snapped, "Continue!"

Feeling quite numb by now, Adam continued. "Well, good news stories can also be powerful. It's easy enough to make up a story about people or animals that tugs at the heart strings. Just a few days ago I wrote a story about dolphins being abused, when in reality they were just having a bit of fun. I made it seem as though people were beating them — until they were rescued by the Buro police. I was proud of that story too." He wasn't feeling proud now; his feelings were on hold, to be dealt with sometime later.

A flicker of a smile passed Glenn's lips. He said, "I'm glad you enjoy your work so much. I want to go back to something you said, about having opponents. So tell, me, who *are* these opponents that you speak of?"

That had Adam stumped and confused. It slowly dawned on him that there was a problem with his logic. If the Buro was all-controlling, and all-pervasive, then how could it have any opponents? *That was supposed to be the one advantage of ...* Adam wrestled with his emotions, until he was boxed in by his own thought processes — and admitted to himself that it was ... *a dictatorship.*

Glenn could see what was going on, and said, "Well come on then. Who are they?"

Adam was confused. *Could the dictatorship's opponents be the Red Block? No, they didn't have the resources to mess in the Buro's affairs. It was as much as they could do to feed their own people. So who?* Adam could not find an answer. And then he just blurted out, "The Buro?"

Glenn smiled with satisfaction, and said, "See, that wasn't so difficult, was it? You can't have imagined that the Buro only ever relied only on *your* work — or did you? Not that it matters anymore. So, now tell me what order would you assign to motivators, starting with the most powerful?"

By now, Adam was still disoriented, but wanting to comply. He had surrendered to the situation. He replied, "I know that fear is the only motivator that matters. It's such a powerful force, and people are so easy to manipulate using fear. It can be fear of loss — loss of life, loss of health, loss of loved ones, loss of bodily function, loss of income. But it can be as simple as fear of the unknown or fear of consequences. Fear of being socially ostracised etcetera. Yes, fear is number one. Other than that? I don't know. Love maybe? I think the instinct to protect loved ones is extremely powerful and can obviously be used to manipulate people."

"How so? Elaborate please."

"Well, most people will do anything to protect their loved ones if they have any, so they will act in ways that they don't normally act, just to protect them. It could be direct threats — or blackmail, like 'unless you do this, I'll do that'. Or it could be more subtle than that. Making someone believe that their action is necessary to protect their people. Or setting things up so that they believe that their loved ones have done wrong, and need to be protected through illicit action."

Adam was floundering, trying to invent possible scenarios, and Glenn became aware that this line of prodding was going nowhere, so he said, "Let's get back to fear. Tell me more."

Almost by instinct, Adam's heart missed a few beats. He was afraid of Glenn. And he was afraid of what awaited him. His palms started sweating. He replied, "Yes. Well, I think fear is the most powerful motivator. Maybe because most people want to feel safe. For sure, fear is nature's way of keeping them safe, keeping them away from danger. They want their lives to be predictable, to have a routine. So people will give up a lot just to feel safe and secure, and anything that jeopardises that is seen as a real threat. People react to threats in different ways. They might bury their heads in the sand and pretend it doesn't exist. People are willing to turn a blind eye to all sorts of things to maintain their sense of security.

But if you force them into a corner, then sometimes they might plan for the worst. Or become defiant."

Glenn interrupted with, "Ah, but what about adventure? People want adventures, do they not? How can they sense excitement if they are constantly afraid?"

A deep weariness overcame Adam. He had never thought about having a sense of adventure. He had no way of relating to it. He didn't understand the real meaning of it, much less the thrill of it. He mouthed the words, and watched himself say, "I don't know anything about that."

Glenn stared at him for a while before saying, "OK, well, your loss. So what do you do if people don't respond to fear?"

Adam no longer believed in the world his words implied. He no longer cared, and he was emotionally exhausted from constantly being afraid, so he just went through the motions of saying, "Well, you just have to frighten them more. Make the threat so overwhelmingly fearful that they despair at their impotence. Then they might keep their heads down."

"And if they don't?"

"I guess that's why we have people like you and your colleague."

Glenn reacted like a hawk, suddenly focussing intensely on Adam, who immediately realised that he had taken his comment as an affront, an insult. Adam was shocked at his brittleness, wondering *'How do the Buro leave people like this in positions of real power over others? Does anyone even care?'* And Karl, who up to now had showed no emotion, fixed on Adam's face with obvious disapproval. Without another word, Glenn nodded to Karl and they left the room. Adam knew that whatever had just happened, it wasn't good.

After a while, he got up and tried the door, but as he expected it wouldn't respond to his presence. He became increasingly afraid and his feet felt like blocks of ice — cold and numb.

How long will they leave me here? What have they decided? Have they gone away to discuss what to do with me? Do I still have my job and everything that goes with it?

He needed to pee, but held on to it. Then, after an hour or so the door silently opened and a slender middle-aged woman with a shock of black hair entered the room. "You are now free to go," she said, "I will show you the way out if you'd like to follow me." She led him back the way he'd come, to the lift. The lift door slid open, and then closed behind them. When the doors opened again, it seemed to be the same place he'd been brought to earlier, except now there was an unmarked taxi of unusual design parked near the lift doors. She pointed to it and said, "You may take this PDTM. It belongs to the Buro and already knows of your journey. You will have thirty minutes to vacate your apartment. Thank you for your attendance today."

8

Adam wasn't sure he had heard right. He said, "Pardon? Can you say that again?" But the woman was set on her path and had already re-entered the lift. With a shock, Adam realised that she was a bot. A very good bot, but definitely a bot. His feet were still freezing cold. Almost in a trance, he got into the PDTM and it drove out of the car park into broad daylight, onto Victory Street and towards his place. He had lost all track of time, and his mind was struggling to accept what the bot had said. He badly needed to pee. And then could no longer hold it in. He suddenly let go and tried in vain to keep his robe from getting wet. His feet were warmed by his urine, and relief flooded over him, but he felt utterly humiliated. As the PDTM pulled up outside his apartment block, the door swung open. He climbed out and headed up the front steps. It was still very early in the morning, just after dawn in fact, so there was only a smattering of people around. But he did attract a few stares as he went. One man stopped in his tracks and gave Adam a very disconcerting look, almost as though he realised Adam's predicament but strongly disapproved. By the time he got to the top step, his feet were no longer leaving wet footprints behind. The front doors swung open and he crossed the foyer and then took the lift. No problem there. His apartment door slid open to give him access and he made a beeline for his office to look at his messages. His screen recognised his approach and lit up immediately with the following message, which it simultaneously spoke:

"Thank you for your many years of service. Once you leave this apartment, you will no longer be an employee of the Buro. You have thirty minutes in which to vacate. Should you fail to vacate within the allotted time, you will be incarcerated for an indefinite period."

Adam was stunned, and just stood for a moment before a shattering dismay set in. He didn't know what things to take with him. Everything belonged to the Buro. His screen, all of his technology. *Think straight!* None of that was any use to him now. Clothes! He had to take clothes. He looked at his watch and knew he had enough time for a badly needed shower — it might be his last opportunity for a while.

He towelled himself afterwards and chose to wear jeans, walking boots, a T shirt and a waterproof jacket. He might be a bit too warm, but that was better than being cold. He then picked his best backpack and filled it with more jeans, a heavy jumper, some shaving gear, more T shirts, socks and jocks. Glasses! He nearly forgot them. He went to get them from the coffee table where he'd left them. He realised he would need a hat too, so he went back to his walk-in robe and picked a felt fedora and put it on. He looked at his watch. He had six minutes left. He searched around for inspiration, but none came. His heart felt unbelievably heavy as he took a final look and left it all behind. He slowly descended the stairs, crossed the foyer and out onto the front steps of the apartment block. He felt utterly adrift and alone. He knew his old life was over. There was no going back. But what now? He had nowhere to go, no one to see. Another panic attack came over him, and a few passers-by gave him a sideways glance as he crouched over and retched, but nothing came. He sat on the steps and let a few minutes go by. He pondered his situation and got to thinking. His funds were his own. As a well-paid professional, he had accumulated quite a bit of capital over the years, so he could simply check in to a hotel for a few days. That would give him time to make plans for his future. He climbed into a taxibot and asked it to take him to a nearby mid-price hotel. The taxi did not respond. Adam did not know what to do. He just sat there for a few minutes. The taxi eventually spoke. "Please vacate this taxi. You are not a recognised individual." Fear gripped Adam as the implications dawned on him. He had no immediate access to his money!

This was a disaster. Without currency, he could do nothing. There were no longer any local bank branches, as there were no longer any local banks. There was only the Central Bank itself and its Digital Currency. There was no longer any concept of credit, with the exception of social credit — the idea being that if one transgressed, then it was a simple matter for the Buro to direct the Central Bank to selectively disallow transactions at whim. Rumours had long circulated that the bank was simply a wholly-owned subsidiary of the Buro, but Adam knew better. He had researched it in the past, and discovered that the Central Bank was owned by a group of private stakeholders. He could find no information at all on whom these stakeholders were. There were obviously limits on his access to information — for even the most loyal and trusted.

But the first thing Adam needed to do now was to get to the Central Bank so they could resolve his access problems. But there was no Central Bank building in town. He knew that the nearest one was on the outskirts of the next town, Conquest Hill. He'd often noticed it on his travels to cover various news stories. He estimated that it was twenty kilometres or so away. He needed to get there, but the only means available to him was on foot. He wondered if it was even possible to walk that far, especially weighed down with a backpack — it had been such a long time since he'd hiked any distance. The last time was during the Big Black just after martial law was imposed, when he and some school friends had been stopped and questioned. In those early days, there were police and military personnel everywhere, and it just became too hard to be on the streets. How times change!

Adam made up his mind. He had no real choice, so he would do the walk! He arranged his backpack to be as comfortable as possible, and then set off down Victory Street. It all looked somehow different today. He was seeing it through jaded eyes. Buildings he'd hardly noticed before now formed impenetrable façades seemingly designed to keep him out. He soon turned off the boulevard and followed a main road out of town. The buildings became less imposing, and eventually cheap apartment blocks dominated, interspersed with the odd shop. Footpaths became less frequent until there were none at all. He kept going into the countryside, past all the derelict wind turbines and the fields of defunct solar arrays. Nature was encroaching on old farmland with very many trees of various species and girths, interspersed with tangled briar patches and long grasses, so he kept to the road. When the odd taxi passed by he had to step as far off the road as he could manage. Some taxis were empty and some were carrying one or two passengers. He tried not to think about his plight, but that proved impossible as he gave way to despair every so often. But he did manage to stay focussed on his single objective: to get his finances sorted out.

9

After a few hours of putting one foot ahead of the other, Adam started to be aware that the town of Conquest Hill was coming into view. His sense of relief was huge. His feet were very sore by now, not being used to walking any distance, and his backpack was starting to chafe. But his spirits soared at the sight of the town. He knew that the Central Bank was located on this same road, but as he continued his trudge it all seemed so much further away than he remembered.

But soon, as he followed a curve in the road, he caught sight of the bank. It was several stories tall, and almost entirely windowless. As he drew nearer he could make out a sign on its façade stating 'Central Bank', but he'd never had cause to visit and there was no obvious front entrance. So he walked all the way around the building, looking for entry points. But there was nothing! His anxiety levels shot through the roof, so he sat down on the ground to take a few deep breaths and think for a while. He realised he was starting to feel hungry. He'd had nothing to eat since he was arrested at that ungodly hour. He looked at his watch. It had stopped. That had never happened before. Was it also controlled by identity recognition? It was all becoming increasingly depressing. What else would next go wrong?

And then it suddenly occurred to him that there must be a separate building that included a remote access point. So he searched around the building again, focussing this time on the surrounds. He noticed a low structure, no more than a metre high by perhaps twenty metres square, some distance from the bank, but in the same style. So he walked over to that, and then around it. He discovered that the side facing away from the Central Bank consisted of a basement-level tinted glass wall with a paved ramp leading down to it. *This must be the way in!* So he walked down the ramp and as he drew near to the glass, a panel door swung open — obviously for him! So he entered and found himself in a sort of ante-room, perhaps five metres long by ten metres wide. Looking around, there seemed to be nothing there. Just the glass wall on one side and grey concrete walls capped by a grey concrete ceiling everywhere else. The walls seemed to consist of separate jointed panels, so Adam tried tapping them but there was no 'give.' So he turned to look at the glass panel door and tested it with a gentle pressure. It stayed shut. He stepped away, thinking it might need resetting and approached it anew. But it remained inert, firmly shut. Adam was trapped!

But then after a short delay, two concrete panels swung open, and as Adam turned to look, a pair of walking bots emerged. One of them said (with quite a refined accent), "You are not an authorised person. You are required to leave immediately".

Adam blurted out, "But I have a problem that needs fixing. It seems that my chip has failed, and I can't get access to my funds. In fact the system does not seem to recognise me at all. Can you please arrange for someone who can help me? Someone from tech support perhaps?"

This time the second bot answered with a more neutral accent. It said, "You are not an authorised person. You are required to leave immediately."

Adam, frightened by now, said, "But you must have someone who can help me. It's just a temporary glitch, surely? It's my money after all — it's just that I can't access it. I need help."

This time the original bot replied, as though they were taking turns. "You have ten seconds to vacate the premises, or force will be used against you." It started counting down from ten. Adam was powerless in the face of such black and white rigidity and the bots were obviously not open to reason. He turned to face the glass panel again, and now it opened to facilitate his escape. Faced with no other choice, he stepped outside, into a strange new world, without support, without money, without food, without friends.

As if to add insult to injury, a disembodied amplified voice spoke out. "Please remove yourself from the property of the Central Bank immediately. You are trespassing." Adam was numb by now, and in no mood to cause any further problems for himself, so he did as he was bid.

He was now shattered and distraught. He needed to rest and to collect his thoughts. He came across a nearby crumbling stone wall that had seemingly once belonged to somebody. Now it seemed to belong to nobody as it had seen much better days. But he was grateful to be able to sit on it to get the weight off his sore feet.

He tried to understand what had just happened. Slowly it dawned on him that they just didn't care. They had no interest in sorting out individual problems. The obvious inference was that once you ceased to fulfil your assigned function, your life had no further value.

And this bank was obviously just a bot farm. It wasn't set up to service customers at all. They didn't care about customers. Perhaps all bank buildings were bot farms. Maybe that's all they ever were, just a virtual entity set up to handle billions of transactions each day. Adam had to concede that they were doing a first rate job of it. Tens of thousands of bots, all networked together, dispersed all over the western world for reasons of speed and resilience, each forming a small part of a massive overarching intelligence. And probably the equivalent existed in the Red Block countries too, as they had their own currency. After a while, Adam's thoughts turned to more practical matters. Where should he go now? The answer to that was obvious really — as he wasn't really familiar with any town but his own — Victory Rise. So even though he had very few social contacts, at least he had some. He was at home there. And perhaps Penny would be willing to help him out. She might be willing to buy him a meal or two. He guessed that it had taken him four hours or so to get to Conquest Hill, so he should get back to Victory Rise by late afternoon. He stood up and set off, mentally prepared to push through despite increasingly sore feet.

As Adam arrived back in the outskirts, he ached all over. He was just not used to this level of exercise. His legs were leaden and his feet were killing him — and he was hungry. It was one thing to decide what to do, to make the long walk, but quite another to have to face harsh reality of actually doing it. He cursed himself for not having the foresight to take some food with him when he left his apartment. And now he was filled with trepidation. He had no idea what time it was, but it must have been later than he thought as it was now getting dark. Pride prevented him from just asking passers-by what the time was, as he did not want to appear as though he couldn't afford a working watch. He made a beeline for Wilhelmina Block's coffee shop, but there was no one he knew there apart from Wilhelmina herself, and he was not inclined to burden her with his woes. Besides, he had too much self-respect to beg for a meal. He was at a loss for what to do. So he wandered back and forth along Victory Street as it grew darker, thoroughly depressed by now, until he made the decision to seek out a sheltered place where he could sleep the night. There were few people about now, and he was beyond caring about appearances. He came across a classically-styled building with a heavy stone portico, which provided some shelter from the wind and the cold. It was a clear night with no cloud cover, and Adam knew that meant he was in for a cold night. He opened his backpack. Took off his jacket and put on his heavy jumper, followed by an extra pair of jeans. Then he put his jacket back on and tried to get as comfortable as possible, hoping that he would soon go off to sleep.

After a restless night, he woke to the sound of chirping birdsong. He was very cold and the stonework seemed to suck all his warmth away, but there was nothing he could do to improve matters. He pondered his position. The sun was peeking just above the tree line, and soon the gloom lifted. But he was in a state of despair. He could see no way forward. So he just stayed where he was. Eventually a man came to unlock the building, and with a start noticed Adam. He said as forcefully as he could muster, "You can't stay here. Move on, brother, or I'll call the police." Adam knew what that would mean, so he struggled to his feet, full of aches and pains, and moved off without saying a word. His blisters were giving him hell, but he put one foot in front of the other until he was out of the man's sight. Then he just stood there, quite forlorn, wondering what to do next. Passers-by looked at him with obvious disdain.

Eventually he built up the courage to move, and he soon found himself outside his old apartment building. He looked up and pretended to himself that he still lived there. But the front doors no longer responded to his presence, and suddenly he could not stand it. There was nothing for him in Victory Rise, so he headed for the outskirts, just to feel safer and to keep out of the way of the bots. As he walked, he became aware that he was no longer hungry, which seemed a bit strange.

And then he slowly lost track of time as the days went by, without food. He didn't want to ask for any as his pride kept getting in the way, and he realised that he was starting to look like a beggar, unshaven, unkempt and undesirable. He eventually realised that he had to eat or die, so he took to rummaging around in rubbish bins for scraps of food. His misery soon grew into anguish and he lost all hope that anything would ever be any different. He decided that he just wanted to die. To end it all. To have some rest and peace. And he lay down where he was, in utter despair.

———————

He was startled awake by someone shining a blinding light on him. He tried to shield himself from the beam with his hands. Then it spoke loudly in a coarse accent, and Adam realised it was a bot. "You must move on. You cannot stay here. Unrecognised persons are not welcome in the township. Please vacate the township immediately." Adam no longer cared. He just wanted peace and for the world to go away. But it continued to shine the light on him, so out of annoyance he got to his feet and moved off, pushing through his aches. The bot switched its light off and followed him at a distance. Adam felt disconcerted at that, and stepped up his pace, just wanting to get away. Eventually, as they reached the outskirts of Victory Rise, the bot stopped and said, this time with a crystal clear accent, "Do not return. You are not welcome here. If you ignore this directive, you will be incarcerated and then terminated." Adam was shocked by that, but kept walking until he found a bush that would serve as cover for the rest of the night. He took off his backpack and used it as a pillow. As he drifted off, he prayed that this nightmare would all end soon. At least it wasn't raining.

10

Adam awoke to the sound of warbling magpies. He found it strangely comforting and it lifted his spirits. He had not heard that sound for many years, probably not since his childhood. Dawn was breaking and he just lay there, under the bush, for some time. After all, there was no longer any rush. He idly wondered why he had not stayed put when the bot threatened to 'terminate' him. It would be an easy enough death. Adam concluded that perhaps he was not quite ready.

As he lay there, he slowly found his resolve, deciding it was time to face the day. He had no idea what to do, just that he should do 'something.' He crawled out from under the bush and got to his feet. He was pretty stiff, but not feeling too bad, considering. He did a few stretching exercises to limber up, and as he did so, a voice behind him said, "Ah, there you are." Startled, he whipped around to see a tallish strong-looking young man with long, unkempt hair and weathered skin, but quite smartly dressed in black jeans and a black hoodie. Adam was so surprised by his sudden appearance that he didn't know what to say, so he just stared at him, open-mouthed. A half-smile crossed the man's face as he said, "You look like a new outcast, am I right?" and as he smiled, lightly-etched laughter lines appeared, making his face look happy and friendly. His eyes were very dark, and sparkled with humour, and he was probably in his early twenties at most. He gave the impression of being highly intelligent and mature, rare in one so young. He added, "My name is James Julius, but everyone calls me JJ. What's your name?"

Adam felt sheer relief at this human contact as he replied, "Adam Brandon." But as he said it, the name did not seem to belong to him. It was someone else's name, surely.

"Well Adam, you'll have to forgive me for stalking you, but I saw what was going on when the bot stopped you last night. You're going to need help, am I right?"

It was all too much for Adam to absorb. Such a lot had happened but he latched onto the word 'help'. He knew he needed it. So he mumbled somewhat incoherently, "Yes. I don't know. Will you be able to help me? I just don't know anything anymore. Yesterday, at least I think it was yesterday, I had a good job and a beautiful apartment, and now everything's been taken away." Tears started streaming down Adam's cheeks, as he added, "I'm sorry, I'm sorry." And then he let loose and broke into violent sobbing.

JJ was patient and sympathetic with him, as he'd been helping people like Adam for a very long time. He'd seen all sorts of people who'd had the rug pulled out from under them, and some reacted stoically and others reacted like Adam. He said in a gentle voice, "Nothing to be sorry about, Adam. There are plenty of people in the same boat. Look, here's what's going to happen. I'm going to show you the basics of how to survive, and soon you'll wonder how you were ever part of the Buro's world. But first things first. You're probably wondering who I am. Well, I'm a cleanskin, which is what we call people who have never been chipped. I'm not part of what used to be your world. There's a lot of us who live outside it. We try to help people who have been pushed out, like you. I'll explain the basics to you now, and after today you'll be assigned to someone who will show you the ropes. They'll be with you for a few weeks until you're up to speed, and after that whatever happens will be up to you. Once you know your way around, you'll be free to decide what you want to do, though of course you're at liberty to go anytime you like. You're a free man after all!"

Adam was a bit overwhelmed with everything, but he wiped his tears away using his sleeve and managed to ask, "Why? Why do you help people? What's in it for you?"

JJ grimaced, looked pityingly at Adam, and said, "Humanity. Human concern for a fellow human."

Adam felt ashamed and did not understand why, but he felt a response was needed so he said, "Thank you, thank you."

"No worries at all. I get a lot of pleasure from watching as the scales fall from people's eyes. But you must be feeling pretty hungry by now! Here, I've got an orange for you, which should fill a hole! We'll make our way to the others, and there'll be plenty of food for you when we get there. Thirsty?" JJ handed Adam a water bottle, which he gratefully accepted, and then said, "Best eat your orange. You're going to need some energy." Adam did as he was told, peeling off the skin and taking a good bite. It tasted delicious! As he finished it, JJ asked, "Are you OK?" Adam nodded, and JJ responded with, "Right. Then let's go!" Adam leant down to pick up his backpack and donned it. Even though his feet were quite sore, as they moved off the pain was tolerable. He realised they were heading back into Victory Rise, and became alarmed at what the bot had promised was in store for him. His voice quavered uncertainly as he asked, "Are you sure this is safe? The bot threatened me with locking me up and killing me if I returned."

JJ laughed as he said, "They have to catch us first! Really, you don't have to worry too much about them. As long as you keep your distance, you'll be able to outrun most bots." Adam was somewhat alarmed to hear that it was only 'most bots,' and wondered how much he should trust JJ, and how much he could trust his feet. JJ continued, "And anyway, they're actually not that smart. They don't really understand the human ability to say one thing and then do the exact opposite. At least I think that's still the case." He laughed again. Adam resolved to keep his guard up because he suspected he knew better.

As they got into the town, JJ said, "OK, watch for bots and just give them a wide berth. Just stay close to me. People are no problem. Unless you manage to draw the attention of the Buro police you won't have an issue." JJ led him a couple of blocks to a back-of-building external fire escape, and turned to ask, "Are you fit enough to climb these stairs?" Adam looked up and figured the building was ten stories high. So he replied, "Yeah, I'll manage that all right, as long as I can have a rest halfway. Where are we going?"

"You'll see, just follow me," replied JJ. By the time Adam was four stories up, he was out of puff and needed a break, so JJ waited patiently for him to recover before having a go at the rest of the stairs. Adam cursed himself for not being fitter. Too much time spent in front of a screen! But one more rest was enough to get him to the top.

And then, as he stepped off the stairs, quite a sight greeted him. It was too much to take in all at once with people everywhere. The rooftop was a large area with a low parapet wall at the edges. There were perhaps twenty people scattered around, some standing in small groups, and others were lying around, some reading. A few were busy with what looked like handicraft work. As Adam took in the scene, he saw that there were several makeshift tents and some more permanent structures of timber with shingle roofs. And the view from up there was fabulous. He could see his old apartment building on Victory Street from an angle he'd never seen before. From here, it seemed almost insignificant. JJ was watching Adam's freckled face, until he burst out laughing, saying, "I love watching new people's reaction to seeing it all for the first time. Come on, I'll introduce you to a few people. You might want to find a place to put your backpack first. What's in it, clothes?"

Adam nodded, and said, "Yes and a few toiletries." "Goodo," replied JJ not seeming to care. Adam took it off and put it in a handy corner. And then JJ led Adam around making introductions as he went. Adam was overloaded with the strangeness of it all, as person after person extended their welcome, even though he had no hope of remembering any of their names. He was just grateful that he wasn't on his own any longer.

Afterwards JJ led him to a set of garden chairs and said, "Take a seat, and I'll explain everything. Would you like a glass of water before we begin?" Adam nodded, and JJ reached behind for a couple of tumblers, and held them under a water tap on the wall behind until they were each filled in turn. JJ passed one to Adam and added, "Just give me a minute. I'll be back," and he went over to talk to a young man. Whatever they discussed was quickly agreed as they shook hands and JJ came back over to Adam.

He said, "Now, I'll do my best to explain everything. What you see here is how people manage to live well despite being outside the reach of the Buro. There are three or four other rooftops in Victory Rise that are being used like this one, and I guess the same thing is happening in other towns. Sometimes whenever there's empty space in the top few stories, people use that to sleep out of the weather. It's actually surprisingly common to find the upper stories of buildings empty. The alternative is to pitch tents and tarpaulins by weighting them down as you can see. Some people prefer to do things that way.

"So just to let you know about the names we use for various groups, I'm a cleanskin and I think it's safe to say that you're now a 'dark' which means that you're no longer recognised as being part of the system, even though you're chipped. They can just switch you off, as I guess you know already. That means you have no access to anything to do with the

Buro, including money. That's all gone. They waved a magic wand, and hey presto, it's all evaporated into thin air where it came from. So now you're outside the system. No access to Buro services like food, housing, medical care or anything else that you used to need. But if you do get sick, we've got a few doctors among us. And despite the lack of Buro services you'll soon find that you can actually live very well and you won't need anything from the Buro. And after a while you won't even miss it.

"Now, you'll hear some people being referred to as 'glitchers' which means their status is uncertain — maybe they're still part of the system, and maybe not. I'm sure you must have been through a period of that. You'll also hear of the 'untamed' who are sometimes called 'ferals'. They're people who live in the countryside, off-grid, outside of the Buro system. They're just like us, except they prefer life in the country. And that's exactly where you'll be assigned to start with. It's best to learn the ropes and start to understand the dangers from a place where you'll be relatively safe. After that initial period of adjustment, you'll be free to join us in Victory Rise or anywhere else you want to go. That'll be up to you. After all, you're a free man!"

Adam couldn't help but think all these group names were such a waste of energy, but JJ had more!

"So sometimes you'll hear people being referred to as 'freemen', as opposed to 'sleepers.' Freemen is just a collective term for anyone outside the system, like us, and a sleeper is anyone in the system. Us town-dwellers are sometimes called townies, or roofies. Don't worry about trying to remember all of the names. You'll get used to it all soon enough." Adam decided then and there not to waste his energy in trying to remember *any* of the names.

"So anyway, here in town, you might be surprised at the things that the Buro is prepared to turn a blind eye to. A few years back, they tried to stop us from using public toilets. But things turned pretty shitty for a while. Freemen had to go somewhere after all! So they soon changed their minds on that one.

"Then there was a push to stop us feeding off restaurant waste. They forced owners to mash their waste food down into a pulp. All that happened was that the mess created soon became putrid and unbelievably messy to handle. It drove a lot of freemen out of town to join their untamed brothers and sisters, but luckily the effort soon collapsed because it was so obvious that the cure was worse than the disease. So these days as long as we can stay mostly out of sight and not cause any problems, the Buro leaves us alone. We're just another level of society, running in parallel. I find it quite funny that the more they try to control people, the more freemen appear." And then his expression darkened, as he continued. "Though I've got to say, we've been seeing a tailing off of new freemen over recent weeks, and at the same time sleeper foot traffic seems less."

He paused and looked at Adam intently. And then he unburdened himself. "The numbers actually don't make much sense. People seem to be disappearing, and no one cares. I blame too much social isolation! No one cares about anyone else anymore. But it makes me wonder if something's going on in the Buro that we don't know about." JJ looked into the distance for a while with his dark, dark eyes, before suddenly returning to earth and saying, "So tell me about yourself. How did you manage to fall outside the Buro system?"

Adam related his story, keeping the details to a bare minimum and when he finished, JJ seemed lost in thought, staring off into the distance. Eventually he said, "Yeah, something's going on in the Buro. But we can't worry about what we don't know," as his face lit up with a grin.

"So. Tomorrow, someone called Goldie is going to come and collect you and take you to her commune. I'm sure you'll like her. She's great. Her job is to bring you up to speed with everything you'll need to know to survive and be happy. Until then, you might like to get to know some of the others here. I'd suggest you don't wander far. Lunch will be served in a couple of hours' time." And then he was gone, clambering down the stairs. Adam tentatively said 'Hey' to a couple of people, and before long they were including him in the group and wanted to know all about his story, and it was sweet relief for him to be able to tell it, even though he could not resist adding the odd embellishment.

11

As dawn broke, Adam woke up feeling quite disoriented. He'd forgotten where he was, but it all came flooding back to him. He was in a tent. On a rooftop. He was cold, despite being wrapped in a heavy rug. He was suddenly overwhelmed with feelings of desperation. Was this what his life had become, with no hope of anything ever getting any better? Yes was the answer to the first question, and no, there was no hope. This was his life now. So he pulled his rug tight over his head, to shut it all out. He stayed immobile for some time, drifting in and out of sleep. It was Wilhelmina Block's voice entering his consciousness that woke him with a jolt. *She's here!* So he unwrapped himself and went outside to see. A couple of people said "Good morning," to him. He rubbed his eyes and yawned, and looked around. And there she was — easy to spot with her shock of white hair. He walked over to her. She was busy stacking crates of bread rolls and sausages, but spotted him approaching.

"Well I do declare, it's Mr Adam Brandon isn't it? I hardly recognise you with your hair all tousled, what with you unshaven and all! You've always been so neat. I suppose the Buro's decided you're now dispensable?"

Adam realised he probably looked a mess. He'd lost track of when he'd last had a shower, it seemed so long ago, but he replied, "Yeah, it's me all right, Mr Dispensable. But what are *you* doing here? Surely you're not in the same boat?" Wilhelmina grimaced, shook her head and explained that she was in the habit of bringing leftovers to this community every morning, as she couldn't serve them to customers and they would otherwise go to waste. Adam was flabbergasted that she would put herself out like that, and asked her about the risks. She shrugged and replied that if one couldn't look after fellow humans, what was the point of life? A bit of common humanity can make the world of difference to those who receive, *and* those who give, and he was a case in point. Adam felt chastened, almost ashamed, and not for the first time since his world had collapsed. Wilhelmina kept chatting to him as she went about her business, and asked about what sins he had committed to warrant joining the ranks of the dark. Adam simply said, "I don't know," to which she retorted, "Well, you bloody-well should be able to take a stab at it, at the very least. Though it has to be said I'm seeing more and more people like you losing their status in recent weeks. Makes you wonder what's going on in the Buro."

———————

Later, Adam gratefully accepted his breakfast of a toasted bread roll with a sausage, and it tasted heavenly, despite it being his second meal as an outcast — or perhaps because of it. And then Goldie arrived with a bit of an exuberant splash. She obviously knew most people and she seemed very gregarious and popular. Adam put her as being a tad younger than him. She was quite short and slender, with close-cropped blonde hair and a weathered face, as though she spent most of her time in the great outdoors — which indeed she did! She was wearing a pair of holey jeans and a striped tank top. After greeting her friends she was pointed towards Adam, and introduced herself. She poked him in the tummy playfully, and said, "Hey, don't worry Adam. You probably feel as though your world has fallen apart, but we'll soon show you that life can be fun. A lot more fun that working for the Buro at least!" She laughed merrily at her own joke. Adam had never met anyone like her, and he was quite taken with her spontaneity and sense of fun. For the first time for a long time, he felt touched by a ray of hope.

Sometime later, and after Goldie and Adam had said their goodbyes, they set off down the fire stairs. Goldie had to wait for Adam to catch up a couple of times, but when they got to the bottom Goldie quietly suggested that they take the quickest route out of town to avoid the bots. Soon, they were in the countryside, and Goldie became visibly less wary and more relaxed as they picked their way along various paths. Adam struggled to keep up at times, especially when there were undulations to climb, but she kept up a constant stream of chatter, explaining the various aspects of how they lived, until she turned off into some woods. She said cheerily, "Not long now," much to the relief of Adam, as they'd been trekking for well over an hour and his blisters were playing up.

And suddenly they were there, in a small but spread out village, with all of the houses sheltered by a tree canopy above. A variety of small cultivated fields were near the houses and Adam noticed that they were pretty mixed up with a variety of crops. He stopped to take it all in. As if to read his mind, Goldie said, "We try to keep our crops as random as possible, so that aerial drones don't recognise them as signs of civilisation. You'll have plenty of time to get into our way of life. But for now, you'll be bunking with me, over here, and then I'll introduce you to the others." Adam wondered if she meant he would be sharing her bed, and felt his body respond at the thought. She led him to a shingled log cabin which seemed pretty small, and pushed open the front door, which made do without locks and just a simple latch. Adam realised that it was a much bigger cabin than it appeared to be from the outside. It had a proper timber floor, and the windows were glazed. There was one main room with various items of furniture placed about, including a sofa-bed which Goldie pointed to. "This will be your bed for the next few weeks". Adam felt slightly disappointed, but Goldie continued. "You'll need to make an effort to keep things clean and tidy, 'cos I hate clutter. That's my room over there. The toilet is just outside. It's a long drop. I'll show you in a minute. The kitchen area is over there, and here's the shower room and that's pretty much it." She led him outside to show him the toilet, which was a simple clapboard structure. They went back inside and Goldie said, "You probably haven't had a shower for a while, and we're going to need to get you some fresh clothes. Lunch can wait till later. One thing you'll find is that there's no shortage of food — and it's all top quality, grown right here. Loads of veggies and fruit. And we run chooks for their eggs, plus pigs and lambs and cows for milking and slaughtering. We work pretty hard for it, but it's real food, not the processed garbage that they serve up in town! What do they call it? Green food? You've got to feel a bit sorry for the townies, eh? And we've even got a horse and cart to move heavy loads! Anyway, cheer up! I don't know if you're aware or not, but you look so sad. Here, copy me!" She gave a big forced grin which lit up her face. Adam could not help but warm to her — she was delightful.

Goldie took Adam to meet several others, and as before, he had no chance of remembering their names. He was introduced to three other newly dark who'd only been there a few weeks, and asked them how they were coping. Two of them affirmed that it was a big adjustment but they were starting to enjoy the advantages of rural life. The third seemed thoroughly depressed, and Adam decided that pressing him for his opinions would be a mistake.

It was only later it occurred to Adam that JJ had not been back at the rooftop to bid his farewells.

———————

As the days went by Goldie found herself directing Adam's work load, which he didn't mind at all. He found himself increasingly full of admiration for Goldie, as she was just so capable and always so optimistic. They grew closer with each passing day, as Goldie brought out the best in Adam, and they soon found themselves laughing and chuckling at each other's jokes, no matter how lame.

Goldie had him doing things as diverse as digging potatoes (which was back-breaking) and picking peaches. He was exhausted by the end of each day, but he had no choice. He told himself that others were far worse off than him, and while he had no particular skills that were of any use to anyone, the one thing he was useful for was his manual labour. And as the days passed he started to feel fitter and stronger. He realised that his labours were doing him good, and after a few days he even started to enjoy it. It was the first time in his life that he'd spent so much time in the great outdoors. Initially he worried about the possibility of aerial drones homing in on him, but Goldie explained that the bots had a relatively benign attitude to the community. They seemed to regard the inhabitants as an interesting form of wildlife, and as long as they stayed more or less invisible, then the Buro would not bother them.

Adam came to understand that no one was in any way proprietorial about property — it was share and share alike according to need. The community was being run as a commune. Adam wondered how long that could last, as some people's skills were a lot more valuable than others' and therefore the demands on them were commensurately greater. A sense of fairness would inevitably get in the way.

And as the days passed, Adam's feelings toward Goldie deepened, and it was mutual. They were spending a lot of time together and becoming closer and closer. Then one night, Adam was awoken by someone getting into bed with him. Goldie. Neither of them said a word as they became lovers and fell into a state of euphoria.

12

The morning arrived, all sunny and bright. Adam rolled over and drank in Goldie's beauty, for that's what she had become in his eyes: beautiful. She opened her eyes slowly, and smiled, partly to herself but mostly to Adam. He cupped her face in his hands and kissed her on her lips. Neither of them wanted to stop, so they didn't, both getting lost in the moment until they became aroused and made love once more, drinking in the wonder of each other's bodies.

Afterwards, they lay together in an embrace, neither wanting to break the spell. Goldie was the first to break it, by murmuring, "Adam, tell me all about your life. I want to know everything about it. What it really was like. I can't really remember any other life apart from this one. All of my grandparents were farmers, and so were my parents who farmed this land, though they both died a few years back. But you must have been through so much, working for the Buro, being so important and everything. So please tell me!"

Adam looked into her eyes and felt he was home now. This is where he belonged, and everything that had gone before, all the remnants of that past life, now seemed like ghosts that he could no longer pin down. Now, he was willing to try to relate the story of his life. He let out a groan and said, "Where shall I start?" He turned onto his back and put his hand up to his forehead. Goldie murmured, "You could start by telling me what a typical day was like for you."

So Adam did. Details flooded into his consciousness and he felt so safe with Goldie that he kept talking and talking. He was surprised at how easy it was between them. He had been on his own for so long and he realised in the back of his mind that he had been craving human contact for such a long time. He described what a normal day had been like for him, and added context as he went, explaining where necessary the Buro's philosophy and methods. Goldie became increasingly disturbed by what she was hearing, until she suddenly blurted out, "You mean you actually wrote that stuff? You just made it all up? You lied to people?"

Adam was taken aback by the vehemence of her response. He hesitated, but was not about to compound the problem by glossing over it and he didn't want to deal in anymore lies! So he replied, "Yes, I'm sorry to say I did lie. That was my job — to make stuff up! I was a tool of the Buro. If I didn't do it, there were people queuing around the block to take my place … well, figuratively speaking, anyway. I suppose I thought of it as entertainment for the masses. You know, not to be taken too seriously." Goldie propped herself up with her arm and looked at Adam, as though seeing him for the first time.

Adam knew then that he'd thrown the cat amongst the pigeons, but he wasn't prepared to add to the lies. Not to her. He wanted to get everything off his chest, and he was filled with a new-found courage as he added, "You know, making up stuff, lying, is the least of it. I feel ashamed of it now, but I used to deliberately and knowingly use fear as a tool in my armoury. I would create subtle stories that left the reader in no doubt that there was evil to be feared out there, and the only safe path was to comply. Do what the Buro says, and you'll be safe. The Buro will protect you. People can be such cowards that you only have to hint that there's bad stuff out there and they'll fall into line with whatever the agenda happens to be at the time. Looking back, I feel quite ashamed of what I did."

Goldie stared at him for a moment before asking quietly, "And you knew what you were doing all along? Lying and frightening people?" Adam nodded. Goldie sat up on the edge of the bed, facing away from him.

13

For a while, despite that conversation, being with each other was enough, and as time went by Goldie thought less and less about it. But the damage was done, and Adam realised that things between them had changed. Goldie could not help feeling let down by Adam's revelations — he was not the man she thought he was. And as the weeks passed, an invisible barrier between them slowly solidified. Adam started to become discontented, and Goldie sensed it. They still loved each other, but it would take time to fix things between them — and they both wanted to try.

Goldie thought a lot about it, and worried that maybe it was all too much drudgery for his taste, and having to think more about other people, including her, might help things. She thought that an adventure of some sort might help get his mind on track. So one morning on their day off, she suggested that Adam might like to visit an interesting factory, full of machines. She had seen it once before, but had no idea what its purpose was. Adam leapt at the proposition — he was itching to get out and about — so they took a couple of water bottles and set off.

After an hour or so of trekking, the factory suddenly loomed into view, set amongst a dense forest. It seemed derelict at the near end, but at the other end it was apparently under construction. A steel frame had been erected which would at least double the size of the enclosed space, and bots were busy cladding the roof and the walls some distance away. Overall, it was probably two hundred metres by fifty and perhaps ten metres tall. Goldie held her fingers to her lips to indicate they should keep quiet from here on in. She stopped a few metres away from the existing walls to decide the best approach, while Adam scanned around looking for any signs of danger. He could hear a low humming sound coming from the plant, so there was obviously some activity within its walls. Goldie spotted an open window about three metres above the ground. It was hinged at the top and opened outwards, and it had a deep ledge at its base. Even better, there was a drainpipe rising up alongside it, so she indicated to Adam that that's where they should climb up. Then, using quick movements she clambered up the drainpipe and managed to perch herself on the ledge. She turned to help Adam, who followed with a bit more difficulty. Then they turned their attention to whatever was inside the factory, but the glazing was dusty and cracked, obscuring the view in. The humming from inside was louder now, though they could not see anything much. They needed to pull the window open more and slide under it, but it encroached on the same space they were occupying. Adam gestured for Goldie to lie down as flat as possible to allow the window to pass over them, but he quickly realised that the window was quite stuck in position. So, lying on his back, Adam reached inside and gave it sudden pull to open it further and as it did, it made a cracking noise followed by a scraping metallic sound!

They held their breath for a few seconds, but there was no change in any of the sounds from below. They had gotten away with it! So then, trying to be as inconspicuous as possible, they both raised themselves up to peer at the scene below.

At first Adam had no idea what he was seeing. Everything was dark, lit only by skylights above. It took a few minutes for his eyes to adjust, and as they did he realised that there were robots everywhere, going about their business, all different shapes and sizes, and there seemed to be no rhyme or reason to what they were doing. And the interior of the building was just as derelict and grimy-looking as the outside, which puzzled Adam, as it was not the Buro's style. They liked everything pristine and shiny!

But as he continued to watch, after a while the scene below all began to make sense. At the far end, there was a small foundry where legged bots were in control, pouring molten metals into ingots and then before they had cooled too much, other bots were blacksmithing them ready for machining, and then stacking the billets in neat rows. There were also a few metal presses, busy stamping out what Adam recognised as external robot 'skins'. He could also just make out several heavy milling machines, and some small, more intricate machines. All were busy cutting metal and the resultant parts were being stacked separately. Other wheeled bots were humming around delivering parts, which were being picked off by other bots and immediately put to use. Closer in, bots were working on much smaller, highly intricate items which he recognised as being electronic circuit boards and wiring looms. Adam decided that they must be 'bot brains.' And just below them seemed to be the final assembly line — bots were assembling a variety of versions of themselves, and Adam was fascinated to realise just how much complexity went into producing each robot. They were jam-packed with detail, each part nesting with its neighbour and all intricately refined over many years.

The general impression was one of directed chaos amongst the grime and decay, but at the end of the process, bots were raising themselves up and walking off with metronomic precision, one following another through a door below. Adam realised that they were creating and assembling new (and possibly improved) versions of themselves — all without any sign of human assistance.

He had seen enough. He gestured to Goldie that it was time to leave, so she gave an 'OK' signal and they climbed back down the drainpipe, one after the other. They moved away from the factory in silence until they were a decent distance away. Goldie said, "Last time I was here, none of that factory extension was happening. That's all new! The buggers are obviously doubling its size! What do you make of it, Darl?"

Adam was astounded by the implications of what he'd just seen. He replied, "Well, I don't think the Buro's got anything at all to do with that factory. I think the bots are doing their own thing. Some time ago I was given access to a bot factory belonging to the Buro as part of a story I was working on, and believe me, it was nothing like what we've just seen. The Buro's factory was pristine for starters. You could eat off the floor. And it was a highly organised assembly production line knocking out the same designs one after the other. What we've just seen bears no resemblance to that at all. Did you see what was going on below us? I think those bots were freestyling it — building new bot brains while making their own design decisions. Bots developing bots! You know, I'd be amazed if the Buro has a clue that any of this is going on."

14

Over the next few days Adam could not get the factory visit out of his mind, and it wasn't just what he'd seen. He was becoming restless and developing a yearning to be involved again; to matter in some way. After all, he was certainly no farmer. Before long he could no longer ignore the fact that he'd found the visit exciting; it had triggered in him a craving for relevance. He needed to talk it through with Goldie.

But she didn't fully understand what he was going though. After all, she'd always been a farmer and knew no other life, and she was very content with her lot. So as the days went by, Adam struggled to convince himself that it was merely a matter of adjustment. That he'd be fine once he accepted his new life. But then he grew so depressed that they could no longer ignore it. So they sat one night and talked it through again. Things had not been great between them for some time. And by now, Goldie understood enough to know that she had to either support him or lose him. The rot had set in after 'that conversation', so he was probably lost to her anyway and she was expecting the worst. Adam explained that his life felt as though he were in hiding, in a life that did not feel like 'his life'. And that he needed to be involved with the townies, despite the risks. So there it was … he'd said it. It was decided. Adam would go back to Victory Rise. But neither of them really wanted to give up the other, so they agreed to try to see each other as often as possible. They both cried themselves to sleep that night in each other's arms.

The following morning, Adam left the commune and Goldie watched him go. She tried to put on a brave face and managed to hold back her tears, but she was very hurt that Adam didn't look back. As for Adam, his emotions were utterly conflicted — sad at leaving Goldie, but at the same time, very excited about what lay ahead.

———————————

A few days in, Adam was finding it difficult to rein in his feelings of despair. Whilst everyone welcomed him back to the fold, he missed Goldie, and it all seemed so pointless. For a while he toyed with returning to the commune and living out his days there, but he realised that he had to go through this period of pain if he were to make anything of his life. So he gritted his teeth and made a decision to entrench himself in the townie life as much as possible. He soon settled into a routine, which was not particularly arduous. He washed dishes, helped fix the odd water tank leak, collected and sorted food from rubbish skips. He soon came to realise that the bots had their own routines, and once you learned them, it was quite a simple matter to avoid bots altogether. It didn't always help that the rooftop afforded an excellent view of his old apartment block. It was a constant reminder of his past life, but as he got more into his new life, he found it harder and harder to connect with his past.

Then one day the subject of factories came up, and Adam described his experiences at the bot factory. It turned out that almost everyone had visited it at some stage, and most agreed that for sure the bots were doing their own thing by building better versions of themselves, and the Buro knew nothing of it. JJ laughed and said, "You know, the Buro thinks that bots are their servants, but nothing could be farther from the truth. Bots are the enemy of the Buro, and the Buro has no idea! By the time they wake up, it will be too late. The bots will be in charge. Or should I say the bot singular? They're all networked together with plenty of redundancy which makes them pretty much one super-capable entity in any event. You could almost consider bots to be a single living organism. It's just frightening how much power they already have."

The more Adam thought about those ideas, the more worried he became. He knew that he'd had a small part to play by colluding with the Buro. He had helped create an environment that led to repression. He'd helped to give free rein to the bots. None of this would have been possible if people like him had stood up and faced their fears. He felt totally ashamed.

15

One morning, when Adam was doing a food run, he spotted someone he thought he knew, but couldn't quite place. The man was walking along looking into a line of rubbish skips, looking dishevelled and unshaven, though his suit was an expensive one. Then he realised. It was the interrogator from the Buro! Bad feelings welled up in Adam but at the same time he was torn between feeling angry at his previous treatment and a human concern for the man now that he'd apparently fallen on hard times. He approached him warily, and at first Glenn didn't see Adam — but then looked up at him as Adam asked, "You're the interrogator from the Buro aren't you?" Glenn nodded and then experienced a spark of recognition that this was Adam Brandon. Adam added, "You never had the courtesy to introduce yourself, though I don't suppose I cared much about that. So, what's happened with you? Did the Buro no longer require your services?"

"Oh, it's all gone to hell in a handbasket! It's a bit late for introductions, but my name is Glenn Graham, if you give a shit anymore. Look, I was smart enough to read the signs and I got the hell out. I've been hiding out most of the time, and also wandering the streets off and on for a few days now. I can't remember how long really. I tried to warn Karl Petersen … you remember Karl, the big fella? But he knew better. I think he's either dead or in prison. Probably dead. The Buro's been at it for weeks now, replacing people with bots and letting them go. You were one of the early ones and it's bloody lucky for you that you were, because now, Buro employees are disappearing from the face of the earth. I know that the more recent versions of chips allow for self-destruct mode, so anyone born after 2030 or so on can be terminated at will. But I guess you already knew that."

Adam interrupted with, "Self-destruct mode? Really?" He was quite shocked.

Glenn shrugged his shoulders as he said, "Yeah. You must have known. Didn't you? Perhaps you didn't bother to look it up?" Adam was horrified. He'd been so blind, even though he had full access to the Buro's records. How could he have been so naïve? Glenn added, "But I don't think it's the youngsters who are disappearing. I reckon it's the thirty plusses. Maybe the teens will have to wait their turn. Who the hell knowns what the Buro has got in mind for us all. One thing's for sure; it ain't good."

They stood in silence for a moment as Adam tried to deal with this information. Then Glenn said out of the blue, "Look, I'm sorry about what we put you through, but I was just doing my job. You know how it is. So how have you been managing? You're looking pretty fit. I didn't recognise you at first."

Adam came back to earth. Glenn's apology seemed utterly insincere because he shifted topic so fast, and Adam was still very wary. Every instinct cried out against helping Glenn, but he also knew he really had no choice but to overcome his resentment, to let the past go and help this man in need. So he explained the setup and offered to take him to the rooftop. Glenn then broke down and wept, before getting a grip on himself and calming down. Adam almost felt sorry for him. He understood full well what he must have been going through, and his sheer relief at finding someone to help. And there was always the possibility that Glenn might be able to provide valuable information about the Buro.

16

A few days later, Adam was going about washing everyone's breakfast dishes while thinking about Goldie. It had been several days since he'd last seen her, and it was not proving to be very easy to visit her. He was always so damned tired, and it was a long hike to her farm. But he was missing her happy presence, so he resolved to visit her that night. He felt better immediately, and allowed himself to drift into a daydream with her as the star. But he could not help but overhear a conversation going on a few meters away — and it suddenly grabbed Adam's attention. One townie was commenting that he'd noticed that sleepers he'd seen about the place — people he recognised — had gone missing, and in large numbers. He didn't know their names. He just knew that they were there one day and gone the next. And it could not be explained by people becoming dark — there were just not enough newcomers to account for all of the missing. It struck a chord with Adam. It seemed that a lot of people were noticing it. He felt very uneasy as he filed it away in his mind for future reference. He glanced over towards his old apartment building, but there were no signs of life. Strange. A shiver went down his spine.

As twilight descended Adam set off down the fire stairs. On the spur of the moment he decided to head through town. He was experienced enough by now to know that he could indeed manage to outrun bots, and he was curious to see what was going on, with so few people out and about. He saw no one at all until he got to Victory Street, and even there, the roads were deserted. Adam started to get quite spooked, and decided to get off the main street and take the secondary roads. But something caught his eye. It seemed to be a mound of something, just up the way in the semi-darkness. Perhaps workmen were in the middle of some roadworks. Curiosity got the better of him and he walked over towards it, scanning for bots as he went. As he closed in on the mound, he was suddenly horrified to realise that it was a pile of human cadavers. He halted in his tracks, utterly shocked. There were perhaps a hundred or more corpses, stacked on top of each other three deep, fully clothed. He felt shocked, fascinated and frightened all at the same time and he could not resist moving in closer to get a better look. Then he saw her, lifeless.

Penny from the coffee shop!

Her dark hair was partially draped across the fair skin of her face. Her eyes were shut and she seemed at peace. He stopped for a moment and then kept going. A panic attack came on and he leant over to vomit. But nothing came up apart from stomach acid. He took a few deep breaths before continuing. He'd seen enough. It was time to get away. But he was suddenly frozen in his tracks by another corpse he recognised, eyes open as if examining something just above her, her shock of white hair strangely misshapen, as though it had dried while it was wet; she looked very odd with her life force gone. It was Wilhelmina Block.

He was suddenly overcome with the fear that he might be in mortal danger too, so he turned and scurried off Victory Street, walking as fast as he could manage — trying to be invisible but knowing full well he wasn't — until he got to a side street, whereupon he ran and ran, away from Victory Rise as fast as he could manage.

He slowly ran out of puff, and sat on a railing fence to get his breath back. But then he heard a rhythmic pounding. The sound of a bot running! He quickly looked around and saw a lone bot running straight towards him at full pelt. He jumped up in fright, the adrenalin rush overcoming his exhaustion. He put on a spurt to get away, winding between the buildings until he could run no more, dropping to his knees. There was nothing left in the tank. He tried — unsuccessfully — to listen intently as he recovered his breath but after a few minutes he knew he'd lost the pursuing bot. He managed to haul himself back up and sat on a nearby gate pillar. He was still in a state of shock, but despite that he mulled over what he had just seen. He knew that his own survival would depend on guessing right. Who was executing people? The Buro? The bots? It must be one of the two! But that could all wait — he had to get to Goldie now.

It was a moonlit night, not quite a full moon, but the countryside was bright whenever the cloud cover intermittently dispersed. By the time Adam arrived, Goldie was tucked up in bed, though not yet asleep. She was delighted to see him, albeit unexpectedly as they had no way of communicating with each other. She invited him into her bed, and he quickly undressed and snuggled up to her, safe in her arms. She smiled to herself, feeling utterly loved.

But Adam quickly broke their bliss by asking her if anything unusual was happening on the farm. She shook her head, looking at him with puzzlement. So he told her about what he'd seen that night.

She listened intently, and after he'd finished she sat up and said, articulating each word separately, "Oh. My. God!" She looked at him with fear in her eyes, and asked, "What does it all mean? Is it the Buro killing people? Why would they do that? Surely not just so that they can replace everyone with bots? What would be the point? A drive for efficiency? Nah. Can't be. That would make no sense at all."

Adam raised himself on one elbow so that he could see her face in the moonlight. He replied, "Well, what if it's the bots? A few days ago, JJ commented that the Buro thought that bots were their servants, but in reality they are enemies — the Buro just doesn't realise it. I didn't really understand what he was getting at at the time, but maybe he was right. Maybe it's the bots that are exterminating people."

17

In the early hours of the morning, distant roosters crowed just before sunrise. Goldie stirred and asked softly, "Are you awake?"

"Yeah, I've hardly slept a wink, thinking about it all."

"Any ideas?"

"Yeah, I don't think we have any choice. For all we know, they'll be coming after us ferals next. We have to find out what's going on, for our own sakes, and we have to warn the others. That's the only way we're going to survive this. The bots may be doing a purge as we speak, and there's only one way to find out. We have to get back to Victory Rise." Goldie felt afraid at what lay ahead, but nodded a silent agreement, thinking what a brave man Adam had turned out to be. So she told him that, and Adam felt a welling sense of pride.

The sun soon broke above the hills, and Goldie and Adam silently prepared for the trip back into danger. Each was thinking about what unknown hazards lay ahead, and how to avoid adding to the pile of victims. Goldie told the others what was happening and asked them to spread the word. And then they set off, full of trepidation. Neither of them had much to say as they were lost in their own thoughts, dreading what might lay ahead.

As they reached the outskirts of Victory Rise, they both kept an eye out for any signs of trouble, but the town was eerily quiet. They avoided any main streets, and soon arrived at the bottom of the fire stairs to the rooftop. They climbed up, listening all the while. As they arrived at the top, they were relieved to see that nothing seemed to have changed. The rooftop people were busy going about their tasks as though they had not a care in the world. But Adam knew that in reality *everything* had changed, and he was about to spoil their day. But JJ had spotted their arrival and came straight over to them. He had a worried expression on his face, as he asked, "Did you have any trouble getting here?"

"No, but you need to be aware that last night …"

JJ cut him off by saying, "Yeah, we know. The bots are having a purge."

Adam stared back, open-mouthed, and managed to get out, "You already know?"

"Yeah. They seem to be targeting Buro staff and leaving freemen alone, but we don't know how long that will last. We need to be ready for anything!"

Adam replied firmly, "No! It's not just Buro staff. Last night I saw Wilhelmina Block's body in a pile of corpses. I think they're after everyone!"

Just at that moment a shout rang out. "The bastards are coming up the stairs!" Everyone rushed over to look down at the fire stairs, and was met with the horrifying sight of about a dozen legged bots making their way up to the roof. Adam grabbed Goldie's hand and ran, pulling her along and as far away as they could get from the stairs. He looked over the edge, and asked, "How's your head for heights? Because the only way we're going to escape is by scaling the façade. Look, there's plenty of ornamentation to grab hold of. I reckon we can do it. What do you think?" Goldie looked over the edge in horror, and then immediately looked back at Adam, reluctant to take the risk of falling off. But as she looked back towards the fire stairs, she spotted the first of the bots clambering over the parapet, and people were running and screaming, not knowing where to go. The bots were chasing after people and when they caught them they would extend a retractable device to touch their flesh and the victim would immediately drop into a crumpled heap. Goldie looked over the edge again, and knew that they had no choice. She shouted, "We have to go, now!" So Adam swung himself over the edge and got a footing, and then helped Goldie do the same. "Don't look down!" he shouted, to which Goldie retorted, "Well, there's no point in looking up! Just keep going. I'll follow you!"

Every floor had an ornamental ledge that they could stand on and columns were spaced out along the façade, so Adam grabbed hold of a column and used it to monkey down to the next floor and then looked back up to Goldie. There was no way he could help her, and there was no need. Goldie shimmied down the column like a natural, and from then on they both used separate columns to get down as fast as they could, away from the horrific scene playing out above.

At some point the shouts from above faded, but neither of them noticed, as their attention was fixed on making their descent. The final floor was the most problematic, as it was at least a four meter drop to the ground. Adam went first, and then tried to cushion Goldie's descent as best he could. It was good enough, and it flitted through Adam's mind that he should be grateful that he was so fit because of the farm work. Now, they knew they had no choice but to stay well away from the back-of-building fire stairs, which meant they would have to risk being spotted in the street. They made their way from building to building, trying to stay out of sight as best they could, but then a cry rang out. "Stop immediately!" They turned to see that it was a legged bot giving the order, so the pair ran and ran until they had no more puff and collapsed against a low stone wall. As they recovered Goldie spoke first, between breaths, "Jesus wept! That was close! Whose idea was it to come back to town anyway? I don't think I want to do that again!"

Adam kept breathing deeply, and after a while his breaths became lighter. And then he replied, "Oh shit. Oh shit. It's not good. I think the bots are taking over. They may have decided they don't need humans anymore. It seems JJ was right about bots being the enemy of the Buro. I reckon they've been killing people indiscriminately — being human is enough for them to want to take you out. I think we need to get back to the farm, and lie low for a while until this slaughter is over.

But then another cry rang out! "Stop immediately!" But this time the source of the shout was a wheeled bot, so they leapt up and jogged away, safe in the knowledge that it had no chance of keeping up with them. It wasn't very long before they were out of the township of Victory Rise and could breathe easier. They both fell into a silence as they walked. Goldie was desperate to get back to the safety of her home again, while Adam was lost in his thoughts, none of them in any way optimistic. They both realised the chances were that a lot of people had just been killed on the rooftop.

18

As they got back to the farm, there was large gathering of people milling about. Suddenly someone spotted Goldie and Adam's approach, and the pack fell silent, waiting with baited breath for any news. You could have cut the tension with a knife. The pair kept walking until they were at the centre of the gathering, and then Goldie addressed them, explaining what they'd just witnessed. Adam then expressed the opinion that people might like to stay out of sight for the next few days. Most were on-board but some were pretty sceptical. So once the spotlight was off them, Goldie and Adam agreed that in light of the dissent they had to look after themselves, first and foremost. They would have to make their own decisions about what was best for them. Neither could guess what would happen in the coming days, and they knew that they had to be prepared for anything.

———————

A few days went by and Adam became increasingly disconsolate. So he made sure he kept busy enough to occupy his mind, and there *was* plenty to do on the farm. Goldie had shut Victory Rise out of her mind and tried to pretend to herself that the massacre had not happened. It was just a bad dream. But she worked alongside Adam because she instinctively knew that he needed her.

They were just starting to think about their dinner as twilight descended. Goldie was first to hear approaching footsteps, and then someone suddenly shouted out, "Anyone in?"

It was JJ! They were both excited, relieved and so happy to see him! He did look somewhat the worse for wear as he said, "I hoped like hell I'd find you both here. Thank God you've survived. What a bloody horror show it's been! How on earth did you get away? I completely lost track of you. One minute you were there and the next minute ... chaos!"

Adam explained that they'd managed to shimmy down the façade. JJ looked blankly at them and said, "Oh. I didn't think of doing that at the time."

"So how did *you* get away then?"

"I stopped trying to escape. I was knocked over by someone who fell on top of me, so I just stayed put and played dead. The poor bugger on top of me wasn't playing dead. I knew him pretty well — same as you probably. His name was George." He went silent for a few seconds. Adam had indeed known George — he was always helpful and cheery, and knowing he was dead just added to the horror. JJ continued, "I was holding my breath as best I could, by filling my lungs and hanging onto it as long as possible. I let it out as slowly as I could. After the killing was all over the bots just left. I don't know if they planned to collect us later, or if they were just going to leave us there. Maybe they were just going to leave the bodies for the crows. I don't know."

"So what happened then?"

"Well, once they'd gone, I managed to get out from under George — and lucky for me it was *only* his body on top of me, otherwise I might have had problems breathing — so anyway then I checked for any other signs of life ... " JJ took a few deep breaths. He was struggling to keep calm. "But there were none. I was the only one. So I listened for a few more minutes and then took the stairs to the bottom. But there were bots everywhere, so I had to keep on hiding for a time before moving on. I took the risk and checked out Victory Street, and all there was to see were piles of dead bodies stacked up three of four deep, with no sign of any human life anywhere. Just dead bodies all over the place."

Goldie was feeling hollowed out with all of the trauma and just wanted it to stop. For the world to go back to how it was. Adam was thinking through the implications. JJ calmed himself, and added, "Well, if there was any doubt before, there's none now! This is a complete takeover by the bots. They don't need humans anymore. And what's even more galling is that the Buro was stupid enough to collude in its own destruction by continually replacing employees with bots."

Goldie spoke up. "You know, maybe the bots won't care about us untamed, and I'm including both of you because we're all ferals now. The bots or the Buro or whoever always seemed to turn a blind eye to us. I think they thought of us as a harmless form of wildlife. After all, they haven't tried to eradicate any other species."

Adam and JJ were both thinking the same thing. Was it the Buro who kept the untamed out of harm's way, or was it the bots?

Adam said, "I'm sure we'll find out soon enough. But you know, with the benefit of hindsight I kept on missing the signs. I'm sure that bots became self-aware a while back, and as soon as that happened, they were always going to decide that humans were a problem. We're too unpredictable and erratic for their flawless logic. We're much too messy for them."

Goldie, practical as ever, said, "I suppose we need to work it out as we go. Will the bots be coming after us or not? We won't know unless and until they do decide to. Until then, we should just be very wary.

19

One morning, a new arrival turned up at the farm. She was in her mid-twenties and quite curvaceous with shaggy blonde hair, and a cute face. She was wearing a bold black and white patterned top underneath a black leather jacket, blue jeans and sneakers, and it was pretty obvious from the state of her clothes that she'd been sleeping rough for a while. She seemed vaguely familiar to Adam. She had a spaced-out expression as though she were in a trance, and as she neared them, Adam called out, "Do you need help?" and the woman suddenly burst into tears of relief, saying between sobs, "Oh my God, I can't believe it. You really are *people*." She got closer and suddenly embraced Adam, hanging on to him tightly. She explained, "You'll have to forgive me. I just need a hug! It's just that I haven't seen anyone else for ages." She released Adam from her clutches and hugged JJ, as she said, "I thought I might be the only one left alive. I'd heard about this farm, so I tried to find you, but I got completely lost! But you're really here! Alive! I'm so relieved!" She released JJ, and thanked him for his tolerance.

"So what do we call you?" asked Goldie.

"Andrea. Andrea Carver. What are your names? How did you all manage to escape the massacre?"

They all made their introductions, and then Adam explained their story. As he finished, he asked, "So, Andrea, what's your story? How did you manage to escape?" Tears kept rolling down Andrea's cheeks, as she was so happy to find the trio, but she managed a giggle or two in amongst the tears. "I don't know where to start." But once she did start, there was no stopping her.

"Things were getting worse for the last few weeks. That was when people started disappearing. At first I didn't notice but then I did. It seemed to be mainly

Buro staff. I thought they were just downsizing, no biggie. I was working at Wilhelmina's coffee shop, do you know it? You know, I reckon I've seen you before, Adam. Were you ever one of our customers?" Adam smiled and nodded as Andrea smiled back and continued, "Ah, I thought so. I graduated recently, and I was filling in time at the coffee shop while waiting for a suitable position to come up, as you do! Anyway, a few weeks ago — or was it less? I've lost all sense of time. Doesn't matter. That morning. While I was working, I saw an assembly of robots moving up Victory Street. I'd never seen that before. It made no sense. So I kept my eye on them and then as they came closer I could see that they were attacking people. Just ordinary people. Grabbing them. I think they were electrocuting them. They were falling down where they stood, and I think now they must have been killed. I don't think anyone in the shop noticed what was going on, but I sure as hell did, so I shouted a warning and got the fuck out of there. I just dropped everything and ran. And then there were formations of bots marching down the streets, everywhere. I didn't dare go back to my place, so I just kept running until I hit the outskirts of town. There are no robots out there, so I hid behind a bush. I spent the night there, and in the morning I was pretty hungry, so I snuck back toward the coffee shop where I knew there was lots of food, and there were just bodies everywhere. Everywhere. People I knew. People I worked with." Tears ran down her cheeks and she took a few deep breaths before continuing. "When I got to the shop, they'd cut the power so the fridges had stopped working. They haven't worked since. I think the power's off everywhere."

Adam interjected. "If there's no power, surely the bots can't operate indefinitely?"

JJ cut in and said, authoritatively, "Different topic. There's actually plenty of theories about that and we can discuss it later. Let's hear what Andrea's got to say first."

Andrea said, "Well, that's about it really. I've been living off cakes and cold meats and salad, and when that ran out, stale bread, and then tins of beetroot and corn and stuff. It was so lonely and I just decided to get away from Victory Rise and see if I could find any other people. I'd heard this farm existed, but I didn't know where it was, and I got completely lost. I was losing hope, and I hate to admit it, but I'd decided to end it all somehow. I just didn't have the courage to do it. And now, I'm very glad I didn't." She beamed a big smile at the others.

Adam turned to JJ and said, "So, what's this about bots not needing power?"

JJ replied, "Well, it's just a theory. For a long time people have wondered how bots are able to keep going. I don't think anyone's ever seen them being charged — not that I'm aware of at any rate. One theory that makes some sense is that there's a permanent EMF field in operation, sort of like a wireless charging device."

For a tiny moment Adam felt frustrated that he no longer had any access to the Buro's research systems, but he instantly realised how unlikely it was that the Buro still existed *at all*, let alone its systems. Overshadowing everything was the knowledge that bots must have taken over all of the cities and exterminated all human pests from them.

20

At first, things went well enough with Andrea. Everything was new to her, and she took delight in the simple physicality of life on the farm. But as the weeks went by she became quieter and more withdrawn. Things came to a head when Goldie came across Andrea, on her own, quietly sobbing. Goldie sat alongside and put her arm around her, saying nothing. She rightly guessed that Andrea needed comfort and would talk in her own time. And then after a while went by, she did. "I'm so sorry, Goldie. I'm just feeling a bit overwhelmed with everything. Everyone I knew is dead, and I'm just finding it so hard, so hard. My parents are dead, my grandparents are dead. My friends are dead. And no one's coming back. And I look at my life. Is this really all there is? A life of hard physical work until I'm worn out and die?" She sobbed some more, and then added, "I just miss my old life so much."

Goldie understood that she was feeling the loss of friends and family, but had no way of relating to her worries about her new life. It was all Goldie had ever known, and death and destruction aside, she was content to shut all of that out and just live her life out on the farm. But she knew enough to know that talking might help, so she made it clear that she was happy to sit and listen. She got her started by saying, "So, tell me about your old life. All about it, especially the best bits!"

Andrea grimaced and replied, "I know what you're doing. You don't need to listen to me drivel on about my life. It's very kind of you and all, but..." Her tears started to dry up. She rubbed her cheeks and turned to look at Goldie and said, "It's just, or at least partly the loss of my dreams. A few weeks ago I had it all to look forward to. I loved being a qualified software engineer, and it was all so exciting applying for jobs. Never knowing what lay ahead, but knowing it was only good things. Or mostly good things anyway."

Goldie felt out of her depth, and covered it by managing to say, quite cheerily, "Well no point living in the past. Not while there's fruit to be picked and veggies to be plucked!"

———————

That night in bed, Goldie told Adam of the conversation. His interest was piqued the instant he found out that Andrea was a software engineer. From that moment, his mind became abuzz with ideas and possibilities. He became convinced that there must be some way of capturing a bot and reprogramming it with a virus. He hardly slept that night as he was so excited, and the night simply flew by. After what seemed to Adam like an impossibly short time, daylight gradually imposed itself, casting a gentle misty light until the sun peeked over the horizon and quickly lit up the sky. Goldie slowly awoke. She rolled over to face Adam and said sleepily, "Good morning babes. What *was* it with you last night? You were tossing and turning all night!"

"I'm sorry honey, but as soon as you told me that Andrea is a software engineer, I've been busy planning and thinking through problems in my mind. I've been tossing and turning all sorts of ideas around

— and now I reckon I've got the bare bones of a workable plan."

"Would you like to tell me about it?"

Adam could hardly contain himself, and excitedly rushed out his ideas, one spilling over the next until Goldie stopped him cold. "Wait, wait. I'm just not following you. You're not making any sense. *And* I'm only half-awake. Why don't you slow down and take the time to collect your thoughts? In fact, better still, why don't you explain your ideas to the other two over breakfast?"

Goldie showered first, and when she returned, found Adam fast asleep, obviously feeling utterly exhausted. She decided to let him sleep, and started to cook herself a light breakfast. She was soon joined by Andrea and JJ, so she cooked for them all. And suddenly, Adam appeared in the bedroom doorway, rubbing his eyes. "I thought you were out for the count, darling," said Goldie. "Are you sure you've had enough sleep?"

"Yeah, I won't be able to get back to sleep now. I need to tell you all about my plan." He quickly explained what he was thinking. At first Andrea thought the idea totally impractical, but the idea appealed to JJ's sense of adventure. He became pretty excited at the idea of being the ones to bring down the bots, and he pressed Andrea as to what steps would be needed to carry it out.

Andrea pointed out that it was all ifs, buts and maybe's. Even if you could capture one, you still had to understand enough of the operating system to work out how to reprogram it — no mean feat in itself! But she conceded that it might actually be possible, which excited both JJ and Adam. Andrea became lost in her own thoughts, trying to assess whether she would have the skills to reprogram the bots.

Goldie's was the only voice of caution. She was against the idea, as there were too many unknowns, and really, what would a world without bots achieve? Life would be no different. They would still have to farm and try to enjoy life. But she was a lone voice as Andrea started to change her tune and see it as a technical challenge worthy of her skillset. So Goldie went along with the others as they started to plan.

The first step would be to capture a bot, and an older generation of bot with wheels seemed the obvious route to take, as you would just have to knock it over and constrain its arms to prevent it from righting itself. Then it would have to be brought back to the farm for Andrea to work out how to crack the operating system. It would take the two men to pull it off, one to knock it over and hold it down while the other bound its arms. They decided the best way of getting it back to base would be by using a horse and cart. They would need to discuss that part of it with the other farmers to get their agreement. That would be one of the major hurdles to overcome: selling the idea to the others. So they put the word out that a meeting was being convened that afternoon to discuss a plan to capture a bot.

21

As the day wore on, Adam became increasingly nervous. He knew that the meeting would be 'make or break.' JJ was just plain excited, while Goldie was worried and Andrea was lost in her own thoughts. Mid-afternoon arrived, and people started coming in dribs and drabs to attend the meeting. Adam soon decided that the likely attendees were all there, some thirty or so people, so he called for their attention and made his little speech that he had been preparing.

"Fellow farmers. As you know, robots and AI in general pose an ongoing threat to us all. You will be aware that the Buro is no more. Instead, we have robots who have used violence to take over. They have killed people. Large numbers of people. There are no longer any inhabitants of our towns and cities. We, and others like us are the last humans. But it may not end here. We do not know what plans the bots have for us. It is possible that they intend to eradicate all human life. We simply don't know. But what we do know is that we cannot simply allow that to happen. We need to fight back, using whatever means are at our disposal. Now, we have worked out a plan to fight back. We believe that bots have a vulnerability that we can exploit, to fight back. That vulnerability is a vulnerability to viruses. Just as we humans can be infected by viruses, so too can robots. And because they are all networked together, a single virus can spread to encompass all bots on the network. So, what can a virus achieve? At best, it can render all bots on the network completely useless. They stop working. They become incapable of doing us any further harm. So what is our plan? Well, we plan to capture a bot. Now you might well think 'that's impossible!' But we're planning to capture a wheeled bot as they are physically the easiest to upset, to get off balance and tie down. And then, to work out a way to infect it with a fatal virus. A virus that will spread across the world and make us free again! We are very lucky to have Andrea Carver on board. She is a fully qualified software engineer who has a good chance of pulling it off. But we also need your support. We need to borrow a horse and cart, to transport the bot back to the farm where we can work out exactly how to infect it. So! Will you vote in favour? Let's see a show of hands!"

Adam was worried that he'd overwhelmed his audience with grand themes of death and destruction when all he wanted to do was borrow a horse and cart. But his worries were needless. A few people grumbled and muttered, but a few hands went up, and then a few more until almost all had their hands raised. Adam breathed a sigh of relief and then asked for a couple of volunteers to help capture a bot. This time, plenty of hands shot up, and Adam picked a couple of strong and fit looking blokes. Dave and Noah. He thanked his audience. Goldie put aside her worries and was filled with admiration at how well he'd handled it. He'd come so far in such a short time, and she worried that he was now out of her league. He seemed so self-possessed and in control. So fearless.

And now, JJ was full of excitement at having the nod to putting their plan into action, and Andrea was filled with trepidation. It was all on her! She hoped like hell that she would measure up.

———————

After the group dispersed, they sat and made plans for the following morning. The men would go on their own with the horse and cart to the outskirts of Victory Rise, find a place to tie up the horse, and then look for a suitable wheeled bot on its own, well away from other bots. Adam, JJ and the two volunteers discussed at length how best to get the bot off balance and quickly tie its arms. The best way seemed to be using a rope lasso. Then they had a few practice runs until they were satisfied with their techniques. They felt ready!

———————

Dawn broke, and the men set off with the horse all bridled up, cart in tow. They kept mostly silent as they trudged along the rough dirt track, but as soon as they got to the road that led to Victory Rise, they had to contend with the odd passing taxibot. As they made their way along the road Adam found the sight of all the broken windmills very depressing — a reminder of how easy it can be to lead people astray — though JJ seemed oblivious to it all. Before long, they reached the outskirts of the town, so they started looking for a suitable place to tie up the horse. A fire hydrant did the trick. Now for the hard part — finding a wheeled bot on its own! The four kept silent as they made their way into the town, keeping to the edges, pausing before moving on, using trees to screen their progress. Before long they had arrived in the Victory Street area, and their difficulties in remaining hidden now multiplied. There were certainly plenty of wheeled bots to choose from, but they were all in visual range of each other. They were going to have to take risks. Adam signalled the others to stay put and wait for a likely bot to pass by. Adam hid behind a portico column while the others chose a façade recess. Whilst their view out was not the best, they had a great view of Adam who could signal them if a bot approached.

And then they waited. And waited. And waited some more.

They were all becoming increasingly restless as the time went by. JJ was wondering just how organised the bots were — maybe they only travelled on predefined routes and this wasn't one of them. Adam toyed with the idea of giving up. Packing it in. He told himself to give it ten more minutes. And then it happened! No one was ready for it. A wheeled bot was heading right between them, so Adam leapt up and rushed at it, knocking it over with a rugby tackle. Dave and Noah pinned its arms down, while JJ almost missed the opportunity, but managed to slip his lasso around the bot, pulling it tight and knotting it. The bot struggled and strained against the rope lasso but to no avail. Adam grabbed the wheeled end while JJ picked up the 'head' end, and they ran as fast as they could manage, away from the Victory Street area, towards their horse and cart. It was quite a struggle as the bot kept straining against the ropes, moving as much as it could with sudden jerky movements, and it *was* quite heavy. They arrived at the fire hydrant soon enough.

But there was no horse! Their hearts sank. Surely it hadn't been taken! They looked around desperately. It occurred to JJ that the horse may have sought something to eat, so he scanned around looking for greenery, and there it was! Nibbling away at a tree's leaves! So the four of them staggered over and lifted the bot onto the cart and then headed back the way they'd come without further delay. It was only when they got to the dirt track that they allowed themselves a breather and a shared word of congratulation.

22

As they arrived back at the farm, Goldie squealed with delight when she saw that they'd accomplished their mission. Andrea was less delighted because she knew that now, everything was on her shoulders. It was make or break time. The men lifted the bot off the cart, and then JJ took the horse and cart back. Dave and Noah decided they'd done enough and returned to their farms. Andrea examined the bot, which was no longer showing any signs that it was prepared to struggle, and she decided that they would need to disassemble its arms so that it could no longer pose any threat. Adam agreed that that was the sensible thing to do, and once JJ got back, they set to work. It proved to be a complicated undertaking, and needed a full set of standard tools. Of course, the farm had them for working on agricultural machinery, including very small tools and it was a simple enough matter to borrow them as it was all common property.

Word got around, and over the next few days, most other farmers came to sightsee. Goldie fronted them to keep the pressure off the others, but even so, several days passed before they had managed to remove the arms. Now, it was all over to Andrea. No one else could help. Days turned to weeks as Andrea became obsessive with her task. She had the bot in all sorts of pieces, exposing the electronics which was her sole focus. No one wanted to question her about progress. They knew instinctively that she needed to live in her head for a while.

One fine morning, Andrea had a huge grin on her face as she shouted, "Eureka!" When the others rushed over to see what had happened, Andrea announced that she had made a breakthrough; that she now understood enough about the operating system to be able to create a virus. Another week or two should do it! She could not stop smiling.

And as good as her word, three weeks later she announced success. She had done it! What did that mean? Well, now that she had infected this bot with the virus, it should spread automatically throughout the bot network, irrespective of whatever technical foundation that network used. What effect would it have? It would completely disable any bot's ability to move. Take away movement, and you take away everything. The whole network can think what it likes but if it can't act, it can't inflict any harm. It can't create anything. It can't build anything. It just becomes a useless cloud of thought that no one cares about. Life, such as it is, can carry on as the new normal, without anything other than basic mechanical technology. A step back to the world of 100 years ago.

"We just need to wait a few days, and all the bots should cease to move," Andrea advised happily, sweeping her blonde locks off her face with gusto. The captured bot was put on show for all to see, and it remained totally immobile.

The whole farm became elated as the word spread, and most people found time to wander over to see the static, armless bot.

23

Of course, some of the younger lads couldn't wait, and joined others to go into Victory Rise and see if all bots were truly disabled. But early reports such as they were, were not very promising: the bots were apparently still moving around. Adam again asked Andrea how long it would be for the virus to take effect, and Andrea stated again that it should only be 'a few days'. Three days went by before they could no longer constrain their curiosity, so the four of them, Adam, Goldie, Andrea and JJ set course for the town. When they got to the outskirts, they were all very careful to stay out of sight and not assume anything as they progressed toward the centre.

Their hearts sank as they spotted their first bot in the distance. It was walking along, calmly going about its business. This was not good news! Adam was thinking through the implications. Maybe the virus took time to take full effect. But there was another! And another. The group snuck along, heading towards Victory Street, and saw increasing numbers of bots purposefully going on their way. Goldie was overwhelmed at the lack of people. It was just frightening, like an alien world.

Suddenly a bot caught sight of the group, and shouted loudly, "Stop immediately!"

That was enough of a fright for them all to turn tail and run as fast as they could. Eventually they ran out of breath, exhausted. But they *had* managed to lose the bot. Andrea felt terrible. Between gasps she said, "I've let you down, I'm so sorry. I don't know why it hasn't worked."

Adam started to catch his breath. He piped up, "But it *has* worked! Didn't you notice that all the bots we saw moving were legged versions? I saw no wheeled bots moving at all, did you?"

Andrea felt overwhelming gratitude that Adam had noticed that crucial detail. Her breathing slowed as she said, "You're right. You're right. The legged bots must be using a different operating system, or perhaps a different software version. Shit! I hadn't thought of that. Oh my God, it's back to the drawing board. I'm sorry, guys."

JJ said, "Look, no harm done. We were going to have to disable the wheeled bots in any case, so really, we're making good progress. We're just going to have to catch a legged bot and get you to do your magic on it!"

Goldie was riddled with doubts, but she realised that was her nature, so she decided to just go along with the flow. A new plan was necessary, and it would need all four men, so the group headed back to the farm to fetch Dave and Noah. By the time they got back, they were all tired with all the walking, so they agreed to set off the following morning, when they would be fresh and rested. Adam went to fetch Dave and Noah to ask for their help again. Both were very pleased to be asked, and eager to help in any way they could, so they joined the others to formulate a new plan.

Whilst the wheeled bot had been easy enough to topple, they realised that a legged bot would be a tougher proposition. It seemed that the only way that stood any chance of success would be to floor it from behind, quickly tie its legs together, and then do the same with its arms. The trick would be to sneak up on it unnoticed. JJ, as the youngest and strongest of the group agreed that he should be the one to knock the target bot over while Adam and Noah would tie the legs off and at the same time Dave and JJ would tackle the arms. Then between the four of them, they should be able to carry the bot to a safe place where they could leave it while they went to get the horse and cart.

This time, Andrea insisted that she wanted to come along. The men all looked at each other, and no one objected, so she was in! Goldie thought about it, but decided to stay nice and safe at the farm.

Morning arrived, and after a hearty breakfast prepared by Goldie, the five — Adam, JJ, Andrea, Dave and Noah — stopped by to pick up the horse and cart and then set off. As they drew closer to Victory Rise, JJ took a few deep breaths to prepare himself for what would come next. He said calmly, "We'll have to be very patient. Just like last time, it might well be ages before a likely suspect comes along. For sure, we need it to be on its own, and we'll have to find a spot where we can hide while we wait." So they headed back into town, keeping their eyes wide open and keeping as close to buildings as possible. They chose a spot to leave the horse and cart, this time making sure that there was plenty of grass to keep the horse entertained. As they approached Victory Street, things started to feel too exposed for comfort, so Adam murmured quietly that perhaps now they should find a place to hide in wait. The building they found themselves outside had a jettied upper floor which protruded over a set of columns, forming a kind of sheltered walkway. There were not many obvious places to hide, but it did have a laneway running away from the corner of the building, which would suit their purposes well enough. They would have plenty of warning of a bot approaching, since legged bots made a rhythmic thumping sound on a paved surface. So they sat down, backs to the wall and settled in for a long wait.

_____

Andrea was awakened by Adam shaking her shoulder. At first she didn't know where she was, and almost blurted out a complaint, but Adam pre-empted it by putting a hand over her mouth. JJ, Dave and Noah were all wide awake, and could hear a bot approaching. On its current trajectory it would pass their laneway so all five quickly moved to the other side of the laneway, so that they would be out of sight. Adam signalled that they should be ready for action, and made sure that each had their ropes. His was tight in his hand, ready to lasso the bot's legs. They all spotted the bot as it elegantly thumped its way past the laneway. It took no notice of the four as it was driven by a higher purpose, of which people knew nothing. JJ ran up behind it as silently as possible with Adam, Dave and Noah close behind.

JJ's body slammed into the bot with full force — but it didn't lose its balance. It staggered a bit just like a human trying to save itself, and then whipped around to face the onslaught. JJ tried to shove it over, but as he pushed, the bot just kept stepping backwards, keeping quite upright. It all happened so quickly that neither Adam nor Dave or Noah could get anywhere near JJ or the bot. Suddenly the bot wrapped its arms around JJ. He screamed and screamed in pain, and then he stopped. The bot dropped him and turned tail, intent on protecting itself from further assault. Adam was only steps away as he rushed to hold JJ. He was not breathing. Andrea stared ahead, open-mouthed. Adam lay JJ on his back and performed CPR. He kept going for some minutes, but there was no pulse, and no breath. He smelt burning flesh, and he knew JJ had been electrocuted. He stopped. JJ was dead.

24

With utter horror, Adam realised that he had missed all the cues. How could he have been so dumb? The day of the massacre, he saw bots electrocuting people. And now, he was left in utter despair knowing that his failure to realise that legged bots were weaponised had cost JJ his life. He was overwhelmed with grief. Andrea, Dave and Noah seemed to be in shock, just staring at JJ's body. Adam had the presence of mind to realise that the target bot would probably return with reinforcements. "We can't stay here! Give me a hand with JJ will you?" The men manhandled JJ's body back to where they'd left the horse, and this time she was exactly where they'd left her, happily munching on the grass.

The journey back was sombre to say the least. No one spoke, each grieving in their own way. Adam felt completely responsible for JJ's death, and dreaded having to tell Goldie what had happened. And soon enough they got back. Goldie saw them arriving, and straight away she could tell that something was wrong. But she said nothing, waiting for Adam to explain. And then with a shock she spotted JJ's body. She looked around quizzically, but immediately realised that the group had been through a terrible trauma, so she said, simply, "Tell me whenever you're ready. No rush." She went over to hug Adam, and realised that tears were running down his cheeks.

And then Dave and Noah helped Adam to get JJ's body off the cart and lay it out on some grass. Goldie fetched a sheet to lay over it, but could not bring herself to cover his face. Laid out like that, he looked quite at peace.

The rest of the day was a blur. Word of the tragedy spread like wildfire, and soon a line of people formed, all queuing to pay their respects. Afterwards several of them set to work digging a grave for JJ. Adam finally felt able to tell Goldie what had happened to JJ. It was obvious to Goldie that he blamed himself, and she was having none of it. She told him to stop with the recriminations forthwith! It was not all on him!

———————

The next day they gave JJ a proper funeral. There was a large turnout, as so many people held JJ in high regard. Adam gave a little speech celebrating the life of James Julius. Goldie had prepared the wake with a variety of small sandwiches, and whilst it was a fairly grim affair because JJ's life had been cut so short, there was also time for reminiscing and the telling of tales which lifted the mood. There was even a little laughter from time to time. Everyone agreed that it was a good and proper send-off.

Later, when Adam was alone with Goldie, she knew that he was still riddled with guilt. She gave him the space to talk about it, and he said, "It was mostly my fault. I missed all the clues. JJ was electrocuted when he tried to grab the bot."

"But how could you possibly have known that was going to happen?"

"Ah, when we escaped the massacre on the rooftop, the bots seemed to be electrocuting everyone. And the way Andrea described the day of the massacre. She said they were zapping people. I don't know how I could have been so blind."

"But JJ was there. He saw all of that too. And he heard what Andrea said. It's not all on you at all, damn you. JJ was aware of the risks. You have to go a bit easy on yourself!"

The next few days were difficult. The impact of JJ's death lingered, partly because it was all so close to the bone. And soon, people started muttering about how unnecessary it all was. That if Adam and JJ had let sleeping dogs lie then JJ would still be alive. That if they had ignored the bots, there would be no problem. But others were equally disappointed that the plan to capture a bot had failed, pointing out that Andrea had shown herself to be capable of introducing a disabling virus. And that they were so near to getting rid of bots altogether. Adam became acutely aware that he'd become a focal point, a leader, and that people were starting to blame or praise him for orchestrating the whole sorry mess. He talked it through with Goldie, and her views had not changed. She was always in favour of appreciating what they had, and not to go looking for trouble. But Adam realised that it was incumbent upon him to sort things out, to settle people down. So he decided to seek out Andrea, Dave and Noah as interested parties, but separately, one on one.

He went to Andrea first. Adam quickly realised that she was non-committal and prevaricating. She said on the one hand, it was exciting to be so close to infecting and disabling all bots, but at the same time, was it all too late? The human population numbers had collapsed, and so really, what difference would any of it make? Even if they got rid of all bots, would it really make much change to their lives in this brave new world? And if they hadn't gone ahead with it, then JJ would still be alive. Adam realised then that her heart had gone from the project. And if her heart wasn't in it, it would just be a duty, with the chances of success commensurately diminished.

As he wandered over to see Noah, Adam realised that he might be asking too much of these people. When he got to him, Noah came across as sheepish in more ways than one. He seemed subdued and suggestable. Adam realised that he had not put much thought into assessing his team's character — he'd only chosen Dave and Noah for their brawn. And now here was Noah saying that he would go along with whatever was decided, because of his confidence in Adam. Everything the others agreed would be fine with him. Thus Adam felt the burden of his responsibility to Noah.

So finally, he sought out Dave. Adam was already inclined to give up on it all, and Dave did not sway that inclination. He said that because he'd been a feral since birth, he'd been attracted to the adventure of the plan. It promised to be something different and it had all seemed so exciting. But he hadn't realised how risky it was. And now, because of how JJ died, he was sorry, but he was no longer prepared to take such risks. Adam was sympathetic, and as he left, he knew that it was decision time. He needed to think. So he climbed a small hill which gave him an panoramic view, and sat down on the grass. It was a beautiful aspect. No windmills or solar arrays in sight, just pure unalloyed nature. The clouds were dispersed and fluffy, lit from above with sunshine. Parrots were shooting past in pairs. It was just sublime. Adam soaked it all up for a while.

And then his thoughts turned to the issue at hand. He told himself he wanted to give any plans every chance, so he wracked his brains for ideas. He thought about using a rubber blanket to throw over a bot to form an insulating layer, but quickly conceded that was not a practical proposition. Legged bots had an uncanny knack of staying upright, and could easily shake the rubber off and then attack. He tried to think of another way, another idea, but could not come up with anything that had any chance of working. He reluctantly concluded that catching another bot was out of the question. It was far too dangerous. And without capturing a bot, there was no way to infect and disable it.

But what of JJ's idea that bots might be powered by an EMF field? Adam knew that it was just a theory, and it might turn out to be quite wrong. So, was there any way of testing the theory? Adam could not think of a single one. This was way outside of his expertise and there was no one he knew, still alive, who might be able to help. He opened his heart again to the beauty surrounding him, and felt good. There was no need to worry.

And now, he knew what he needed to do. It was up to him to step up and take the lead. So he put the word out that he wanted to call a meeting to talk about the way forward, for the following afternoon.

25

As people started to gather, the mood was subdued. It was obvious that people did not know what to expect, but they expected something! Adam waited until most people were present, and then tapped a glass bottle to attract attention. A hush came over the crowd. He began. He stated that everyone was aware that the plan to capture a legged bot had failed, and unfortunately had resulted in the death of JJ. And now, a decision needed to be made. Others could pick up and continue with the project if they wished, but in all good conscience, he had come to the conclusion that any plan to capture a legged bot was unlikely to be successful. The odd murmur from the crowd turned into a muttering and before long a voice rang out. "So that's it then? JJ died for nothing?" Adam had no response that would not sound insufferably smug, so he said nothing. A bit of pushing and shoving broke out among the crowd, so Adam took charge and suggested that those who wanted to continue with the project separate themselves to his left, and those that did not, move to his right. Most moved right. And then some switched sides from his left to his right, until there was only a handful of people wanting to continue. Andrea, Dave and Noah were not among them. Adam offered to support those that did wish to continue 'as far as they were able' knowing that the effort would likely peter out.

And so it proved.

As time passed, people began to accept the new reality, and slowly lost interest in trying to change things. After all, their lives were simple enough, surrounded as they were by family and good neighbours, with food in their bellies and plenty to drink. Even wine and beer, which from time to time provided a grown man's way of crying. People began to forget how things used to be, although some made occasional visits to Victory Rise, including Adam, usually accompanied by Goldie. And after a time, the horrors of those fateful days lost their painful edge as they faded away and became distant memories.

If one thought about it, it could be inferred that the bots had won, but as long as boundaries were accepted, the bots no longer had any influence over human life.

Children soon provided a meaning for living. Goldie and Adam had a couple of them, and raised them well. And those children eventually gave them grandchildren. One day, they went for a long walk, grandparents and grandchildren together. The kids were fascinated to see all of the broken down windmills and the solar arrays that were slowly being subsumed by plants, and asked, "What were they for?" Adam deferred to Goldie, who replied, "I don't really know any more. It was so long ago."

On one particular visit to Victory Rise, Adam took the time to remember his life knowing that he would soon be too old to run. As he approached there was no sign of any activity anywhere. He found himself outside his old apartment building. Nothing was being maintained. The building was empty and derelict. He looked up. Most of the windows had been smashed. He looked around and realised that there *were* no intact buildings. He looked down at the paving. The granite pavers had grass growing between the cracks, and they were slowly breaking up. Trees were no longer being trimmed and were out of control. Nature was slowly reclaiming everything.

He surveyed the scene, wondering what it had all been about. And while he did so, it slowly dawned on him that there were no bots to be seen anywhere. He smiled to himself. He had long known that bots had no real point. Without humans, what use are they? What possible purpose do they serve? Humans created them, because humans wanted their help with things. Humans provided their *raison d'être*. Without humans, perhaps they just died of pointlessness.

Adam trudged home, reflecting on the way. He saw with fresh eyes nature's takeover, breaking up all the old useless garbage. In another hundred years there would be no memory of there ever having been any of this, no memories of technology and no memories of the way the world was. It will just be the same as things were in the dim distant past. Life was hard. If you got seriously sick, you died, just as you would now. Your body would be worn out by the time you were sixty or seventy at best. But the pace of life slowed, which was compensation enough, and one could take a sublime satisfaction in the simple pleasures, with all that life offers.

By the time he got home it was dusk with an exceptionally beautiful sunset, lighting up the whole sky with reds, oranges and yellows. Goldie was seated outside waiting for him, glass of wine in hand, utterly contented. She may not remember any other life, but Adam realised that she was all he ever needed. He was happy.

Thus within the space of only one lifetime, there was one more round, one more repetition to add to the never-ending cycle; of civilizational decay followed by its collapse, death of the status quo, and the loss of social memory — leading inevitably to the forgetting of mankind's accumulated knowledge.

But a golden renaissance awaits.

The beginning of the next cycle.

EPILOGUE

As this story is set in the year 2050 it might all, quite reasonably, seem a long way off into the future, particularly for younger readers. But there are elements already in existence that point towards the real possibility that many of the major moves described in these pages are already in train. We may have less time than we think …

THE AUTHOR

Richard spent the first sixty-odd years of his life preparing to be a fiction writer, and now writes full-time. Born in outback Quorn, South Australia, raised in Adelaide, Richard did all manner of jobs in his early years, including grape picking, talc mining, car assembly, waiting-on, ditch-digging and bar work.

In his twenties he decided to pursue a career in the IT industry, based in the UK. He quickly rose up the corporate ranks, managing large organisations on the way, until he gravitated towards international business and variously managed Scandinavia, the Benelux countries, southern Europe, Turkey and the Middle East and Africa, working for American companies, spending most of his time 'in territory' getting to really know and understand various cultures in a way that is not possible as a casual visitor. Richard dealt with 'Oil & Gas', automotive, aerospace and defence, and pharmaceutical clients, generating and closing several major global deals. He learned an enormous amount about how these industries operate, and about the foibles and subtleties of different cultures.

In a complete change, Richard returned to Adelaide in the early 2000's, became a student again, and completed his Masters' degree in architecture. He completed a couple of years' internship before sitting the architect registration exams, and then set up his own practice – only to slowly realise that his heart lay instead in writing.

Somehow or other, Richard also found time along the way to race formula cars, fly ultralights and scuba dive all over the world. He now spends his time reading, travelling, playing the sax, scuba diving and most importantly, writing.

———————

OTHER CRIME NOVELS BY THE AUTHOR

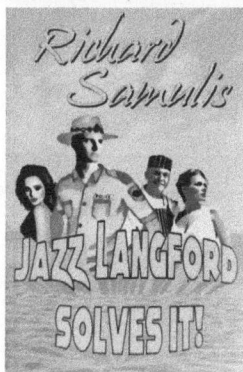

JAZZ LANGFORD SOLVES IT!
ISBN 978-0-9943867-6-2

ONE SUMMER IN GOZO
ISBN 978-0-9943867-4-8

AN ARTFUL REMEDY
ISBN 978-0-9943867-0-0

DEVIOUS
ISBN 978-0-9943867-2-4

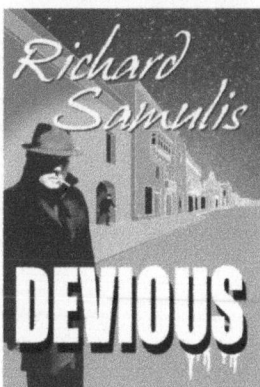